Welcome to the intensely emotional world of

MARGARET WAY

Where rugged, brooding bachelors
meet their match in the
burning heart of Australia…

Praise for the author:

Look out for Margaret Way's
next Harlequin Romance in a special 2-in-1 volume
with new Australian talent Jennie Adams—
for double the romance!

Australian Bachelors, Sassy Brides

December 2009

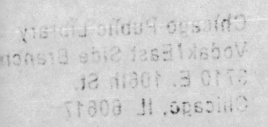

MARGARET WAY

Cattle Baron: Nanny Needed

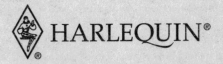

HARLEQUIN®

TORONTO • NEW YORK • LONDON
AMSTERDAM • PARIS • SYDNEY • HAMBURG
STOCKHOLM • ATHENS • TOKYO • MILAN • MADRID
PRAGUE • WARSAW • BUDAPEST • AUCKLAND

Recycling programs
for this product may
not exist in your area.

ISBN-13: 978-0-373-17601-4

CATTLE BARON: NANNY NEEDED

First North American Publication 2009.

Copyright © 2009 by Margaret Way Pty., Ltd.

www.eHarlequin.com

Printed in U.S.A.

Margaret Way, a definite Leo, was born and raised in the subtropical River City of Brisbane, capital of the Sunshine State of Queensland. A Conservatorium-trained pianist, teacher, accompanist and vocal coach, she found her musical career came to an unexpected end when she took up writing—initially as a fun thing to do. She currently lives in a harborside apartment at beautiful Raby Bay, a thirty-minute drive from the state capital. She loves dining alfresco on her plant-filled balcony, overlooking a translucent green marina filled with all manner of pleasure craft— from motor cruisers costing millions of dollars, and big, graceful yachts with carved masts standing tall against the cloudless blue sky, to little bay runabouts. No one and nothing is in a mad rush, and she finds the laid-back village atmosphere very conducive to her writing. With well over a hundred books to her credit, she still believes her best is yet to come.

CHAPTER ONE

A SATURDAY afternoon in late spring. October in the Southern Hemisphere.

Glorious sunshine, vibrant blue sky, the sweet warbling of a thousand unseen birds sheltering in the cool density of trees. A white limousine pulled up outside the lovely old Anglican church of St Cecilia's, one in a stately procession bearing guests to the "Wedding of the Year". As a caption, "Wedding of the Year" was more hackneyed than most, but that was how Zara Fraser, society columnist for the *Weekend Mail*, phrased it at the behest of her boss, a golfing pal of Sir Clive Erskine, the bride's grandfather. Be that as it may, it was difficult for Zara to quibble. This was definitely a *big* society wedding.

Nearly everyone on the bride's guest list was mega-rich; on the bridegroom's side the usual sprinkling of savvy young lawyers with their dressed-to-the-teeth partners, a lesser sprinkling of everyday folk struggling with the kids, the mortgage and keeping it all together. As for the bride's soon-to-be in-laws, they had taken off on a round trip to Antarctica and thus couldn't attend. It had been suggested at a mid-week dinner party that they had deliberately planned their trip to coincide with the wedding because their only son hadn't lived up to the rules of behaviour they had endeavoured to instil in him. Doing the right thing was what got one through life.

What today's bridegroom was doing wasn't right in anyone's book. The word on the street was that the groom had sunk lower than a worm shuffling under a leaf.

Two hundred people had been invited to the church and two hundred and *one* were in attendance. Almost as many more had been invited along to the grand reception. The setting was idyllic. The magnificent shade trees, the jacarandas, the golden shower trees and the apple-blossom cassias were in radiant bloom all over the city, lifting the heart with their splendour. A particularly lovely jacaranda—the grass ringing the tree with spent lavender-blue blossom—dominated the precinct of the old Gothic-style church with its pointed arches and tall slender columns and much admired medieval-style marble pulpit. To either side of the stone building with its token buttresses lay large circular flower beds that literally teemed with fragrant pink roses. A picture-book setting for a picture-book wedding.

To one person at least—the *uninvited* guest—the whole thing was nothing less than a ghastly nightmare.

That person now emerged so gracefully from the white limousine that she appeared to flow out of it, quite mesmerizing to watch. She accepted a hand from the uniformed chauffeur, who couldn't believe his luck that his boss had given him such a plum assignment. The young woman looked amazing—tall, very slender, a vision of female perfection and glamour. Looking to neither left nor right, she moved off in her sexy stilettos towards the short flight of stone steps that led to the church portals.

The wedding guests who alighted from the luxury limousines behind her, however, were frozen in their tracks. They gawped after her, some panic stricken, some downright intrigued.

"Surely that's…?"

"It couldn't be." Shock and a touch of gleeful anticipation.

"She's right, you know. It is!"

"For God's sake!" A substantial matron, Rosemary Erskine, mother of the bride, wearing an amazing electric-blue hat sprouting peacock feathers, gasped, "Cal, you have to *do* something!" She looked to the tall, commanding young man at her side as though if anyone could save the situation he could.

"What's the problem, Rosemary?" Callum MacFarlane, Outback cattle baron and a cousin to the bride, was busy watching the progress of a walking work of art. He had no idea who the goddess was, though he was aware that all eyes were riveted on her. Why not? She looked pretty darn good to him. In fact she would take a man's breath away. Not *him*, mercifully. He had gained immunity to beautiful women the hard way. But there was no harm in *looking*, surely?

Maybe Rosemary was het up because the latest arrival looked dead set to outshine Georgie, the bride? Or was it something far more problematic? The only thing that could account for such a reaction was the ex-fiancée had turned up. He'd been assured that she was behaving impeccably, so that couldn't be it. So publicly humiliated that she was bound to have taken off for the wilds of New Guinea. This young woman was beautifully dressed in what was obviously a couture two-piece suit of an exquisite shade of pink. A dream of a picture hat shaded her head and face from the hot rays of the sun, one side weighed down by full blown silk roses in pink and cream. Such a hat, while affording protection, offered tantalizing glimpses of her classically beautiful face with a truly exquisite nose. The sort of nose women paid cosmetic surgeons a fortune to try to recreate.

The trouble was that most people, unlike Cal MacFarlane whose Channel Country cattle station Jingala was just about as far off the map as one could get, were familiar with that face. They fixated—in the case of the male viewer salivated—on it every week night on television when she read the six o'clock news with Jack Matthews, the long-time male presenter who behind the scenes gave Ms Wyatt a bad time.

"It's that dreadful Amber Wyatt!" Rosemary hissed, her formidable face working tightly. Not a pleasant sight. This was a woman who was known to make people's hair stand on end.

Well, fancy that! Cal had to wrench himself away from imagining what it would be like to have a woman like the vision in front of him. Despite his multiple defensive shields he felt a lunge of desire; swiftly killed it. Euphoria only lasted the proverbial fifteen minutes anyway.

"Hell, Cal!" A relative standing just behind him came to Rosemary's aid. "*Everyone* knows who she is. She's—"

"Okay, okay, I've got it!"

So this seriously stunning young woman with what had to be the best pair of legs in the country was the woman Sean Sinclair, the bridegroom, had thrown over for Georgette. *Would wonders never cease?* It had fortune-hunting stamped all over it. Ms Amber Wyatt had been *jilted*. One had only to be jilted once, never to get it out of the system, he reflected grimly, his mind going off on a tangent. His ex-fiancée, Brooke Rowlands, had played as dirty as a woman could get. Like some knight of old, he had let her get away with it. The betrayal had happened while he'd been in Japan, part of a trade delegation. Brooke had taken a little holiday at the swank Oriental Hotel in Bangkok with one of his polo buddies. Ex-buddy. Ex-fiancée. He might have shaken off what black thoughts remained over that fiasco, but he had no illusions left about women.

No illusions about Sinclair either. He was a fortune-hunter. As fond as he was of Georgie, for her to believe she had utterly bewitched a man into abandoning a woman as beautiful as Amber Wyatt was as probable as her knocking back a previous proposal from George Clooney.

Cal had heard mentioned at last night's family dinner that Ms Wyatt had won an award for a story about street kids, wringing admissions and follow-up promises from the

Government. She should feel good about that. Nevertheless, in coming here today she had flagrantly disregarded the rules of wedding etiquette. How rash was that? And Rosemary had chosen him to be the Enforcer. This totally unexpected appearance was giving quite a few of his relatives a bad case of the jitters. Just when they'd thought the whole thing had been sorted out:

Enter the ex-fiancée.

How could he do this to me? Amber was experiencing a brief moment of wanting to turn tail and run. The malicious gods up there, the ones who toyed with human lives, would be expecting it, but that wasn't going to happen. She was determined on keeping a lid on her emotions, even if this was possibly the most foolish and, let's face it, the most *unacceptable* thing she'd ever done. Gatecrashing weddings was a serious breach of the rules, even for a fiancée cruelly dumped. She put it down to post traumatic stress. PTS was big these days. Even the courts listened.

Giving no outward sign of her nerves, she kept moving in line up the stone flight of steps. This was the very church where they had planned their own wedding. It was unbelievably callous. Sean couldn't be allowed to get off scot-free. For every crime, one had to expect punishment. The bride had experienced no sense of guilt either at stealing another woman's man. That put her on the hit list as well.

There was a shake in her now ringless hands. Of course she had sent the damned thing back by courier. Probably if she'd had the stone checked out she would have found it was a zircon. To counteract her tremulousness, she clasped the chain of her pink Chanel shoulder bag for support. She needed to be as cool as a cucumber to pull this off. There would be some satisfaction in making him cringe. Plenty of women, so cruelly jilted, had been known to run over their ex in a car, then try it in Reverse. She had an idea of herself that precluded violence. But, given the despicable behaviour of Sean and his bride, a frisson of fright was well within her parameters of revenge.

Payback time.

She had just the moment picked out. The *symbolic* moment when the Bishop, revelling in a role he was famous for, began to intone…. "I am required to ask anyone present who knows a reason why these persons may not lawfully marry, to declare it now."

That was her cue to rise. At near six feet in her stilettos it would be difficult not to spot her. Then, when all necks were craned and unbelieving eyes were focused on her, she would calmly turn and walk out of the church, leaving the guests either bitterly disappointed that there hadn't been more drama or aghast at such an assault on wedding etiquette.

All she had to do now was get past the ushers and inside the church. Though she kept her eyes trained ahead, she was aware that her presence was causing a stir. Little whispers wafted to her on the rose-scented breeze.

" Oh, goodness, it's Amber Wyatt!"

"Has she got some guts, or hasn't she?" Admiration there from a sister-at-arms.

"If I were her I'd kill myself, poor thing!"

Come on, why should I kill myself? Amber reasoned. *I haven't done a thing wrong. Wrong has been done to me, just when life was going so great.* God, she felt ill. Buck up, Amber. It won't be much longer. She was the sort of person who regularly gave herself pep talks. Hundreds of them of late. She was dressed to kill. Confidence in how one looked always helped. One couldn't pity her and gape open-mouthed in admiration simultaneously. Her suit was the *exact* shade of pink that complemented her hair—neither red nor gold nor copper but a combination of all three.

"We just have to call this little angel Amber!"

That had been her darling dad, holding his brand-new daughter in his adoring arms.

So Amber she was, though her bright, eye-catching hair was all but hidden by her masterpiece of a hat. It offered a modicum of camouflage. Her accessories were colour co-ordinated, perfect. The whole outfit had cost her way too much money, but her pride demanded she look staggeringly glamorous. She wouldn't have been content with anything less. Her friend Jono, gay man about town who lived in the penthouse apartment above her and charged unheard of prices for writing other people's software programs, a man who could be counted on to deliver a totally reliable verdict when it came to fashion, had given her the thumbs up and a spontaneous, "Wow!"

Ironically, it was her friend, the society columnist Zara Fraser, who had first broken the news to her...

She sat up in bed, bracing herself on one elbow as she made a grab for the phone. She nearly rapped, Who the blazes is this? but stopped just in time. There was a remote possibility it could be her boss. The digital clock on her bedside table read: A.M. 5.35. To make it worse, it was Sunday—her morning to sleep in. It couldn't be Sean, although she hadn't spoken to him for a few days. He wouldn't ring at this time. Sean was safely in London on business, or as safe as one could be in the great cities of the world these scary days. Immediately the thought crossed her mind, she started to panic.

"Hi Amby?"

"Who else do you suppose? Is that you, Zee?"

"Jeez, love, I know it's early. But you have to hear this."

"If you're ringing to tell me you've found Mr Right again, don't dare put him on. I'm not in the mood."

None of the usual infectious giggles from Zara. "Amby, love, you've got to listen. This is *serious*!"

Amber groaned. "They *all* are. Just remember, men aren't to be trusted."

"Ain't that the truth!" Zara sounded very down-mouthed. "This isn't about me, Amby. It's about *you*. Are you still lying down?"

"No, I'm *not*!" Amber swung her feet to the floor. "Spit it out, Zee. There's a good girl."

"Why should it be *my* destiny to have to tell you?" Zara moaned. "Okay, there's no easy way to say it, so here I go. Your fiancé, Sean Sinclair—"

Amber was finding it difficult to swallow. "There hasn't been another terrorist attack, Zee, has there? Please God, tell me no!" Disasters could and did come out of the blue.

Zara hastened to reassure her. "Not something as terrible as that, but bad enough on a totally different scale. Trish McGowan, you know Trish, she's in London. She let me know. I didn't get home until after three. I didn't want to wake you then but I couldn't sleep and I couldn't hang on any longer. Wait for it, girl. Sean, *your* fiancé, married Georgette Erskine, Sir Clive Erskine's granddaughter, at a civil ceremony yesterday afternoon London time."

"No kiddin'!" Amber crowed, not for a moment taking her friend seriously. " I know you like your little pranks, but that's pathetic!"

"No joke, Amby. Proof of what a bastard he really is. This will come as a blow to you, but I can't pretend I don't think you haven't had a lucky escape."

Amber fell back on the bed as if she were taking a long backward fall off a cliff. " I suppose there's no question Trish was having a little joke? It has April Fool's Day written all over it."

"No chance, love," Zara said unhappily." It's October. I never had a clue the rat even knew her, did you?"

Recollections were filtering through. "He met her several

times when she came into the office with her granddaddy. Nothing to look at, he told me. All she had going for her was the family fortune."

"All?" Zara screeched. "He must have started thinking long and hard about that. Listen, give me twenty minutes and I'll be over. You shouldn't be on your own."

Zara had arrived with freshly baked croissants and genuine Blue Mountain coffee. Zara had been wonderful to her. So had lots of other people, though inevitably there were some—like her co-newsreader—who got a warped pleasure out of seeing her suffer such a public king hit. This follow-up wedding ceremony was being held so the happy couple could seek God's blessing. If they got it, God wouldn't be winning any Brownie points with her. It was even possible Sir Clive Erskine had God onside.

The Erskines purported to be a pious bunch. Sir Clive was a billionaire who owned coal mines, gold mines, luxury beach resorts, shopping centres, a string of prize-winning race-horses, country newspapers, and had been the biggest contributor to the Cathedral restoration fund. The bridegroom, Sean Sinclair, was an associate with the blue chip law firm of Langley, Lynch & Pullman, a high profile practice whose clientele included major mining companies, multinationals and billionaires like Sir Clive Erskine. The bridegroom, smart and ambitious, was very good-looking if one found "boyish" attractive. Most women did. He had thick floppy golden-brown hair, dark blue eyes and an engaging whimsical smile. He wasn't terribly tall but tall enough at five foot ten. The bride wouldn't have struck even her mother as pretty, but she was said to be a very nice person, which counted for a lot.

How could that be? Georgie Erskine had stolen another woman's man right from under her nose. Surely that made her a man-eater? No question it was immeasurably better to be from an immensely wealthy family than to be a working woman, however high on the ratings. One way or the other, Georgette Erskine thoroughly deserved the man who awaited her at the altar.

No one better placed than I am to sit in judgement, Amber thought bleakly. *Why can't I hate him? I want to hate him, but I can't.* Her own nature was betraying her. Was it somehow *her* fault? What had she done wrong? Was she too critical? Too ready to debate the issues of the day, instead of falling into line with Sean's play safe opinions? Sean liked to keep his finger on the politically expedient pulse. But she was an intelligent woman with strong opinions of her own. She had even gained a reputation for defending the underdog, the little guy. There was the story last year that had won her an award. Whatever the problem, Sean should have been honourable enough to tell her. He should have broken off their engagement, then waited at least a few months before asking another woman to be his wife. She couldn't have done to him what he had done so callously to her. Sean had only worn the façade of an honourable man…

Late wedding guests, cutting it fine, were still arriving. Up ahead, Amber could see the ushers, decked out in morning suits. Each wore a white rosebud in their lapel. She had to get past them, though by now she was feeling like a clockwork doll badly in need of a rewind. At least they weren't burly bouncers, just good-looking youngsters probably just out of school or at university. They would have been given a list of guests, although they weren't holding anything in their hands. Maybe they would only check on guests arriving at the reception, which was being held in a leading city hotel.

No matter what, nothing was going to stop her getting into that church.

Even as Amber plotted, a few feet behind her Cal MacFarlane considered ways and means of controlling a potentially inflammable situation. He couldn't carry Ms Wyatt off screaming. He couldn't very well slap her into a pair of handcuffs and make a citizen's arrest, but it should be possible to avert a scene. He wished he could see her face properly. She had a beautiful body. Tall and willowy. She held her head high and kept her back straight. She moved as a dancer would. She looked enormously chic. In fact she was making the women around her look *ordinary*, although they had obviously gone to considerable pains over their wedding finery. The brim of the hat was perhaps a bit too wide. It called to mind the picture hats his beautiful mother had used to wear before she ran off with the man he had affectionately called "Uncle Jeff" for much of his childhood. His eyes glittered with the tide of memory even if he had grown many protective layers of skin.

One of the ushers had stopped her. A challenge, or did he want a close-up of the goddess? Rosemary prodded him so hard in the back, he actually winced. "Callum, I beg of you, see to it."

Rosemary, mercifully not a blood relative, always had that combative look. Had he really travelled a thousand miles and more for this? He'd only met Sinclair the night before and had barely been able to disguise his scorn for the man. Whatever Georgie saw in Sinclair was invisible to him. Of course with Sinclair it was all about money. Money was the fuel that drove everything. Follow the money. Way to go. Money and ambition. Sinclair was a covetous guy.

"We just looked at each other and fell in love!" Georgie had told him, her myopic grey eyes full of stars. The truth was that Georgie was overwhelmed to be loved—and had been given the heaven-sent opportunity to get away from her mother. *"I'm so desperately sorry we had to hurt Sean's ex-fiancée but once he met me he knew he couldn't go through with it."*

"Pity the two of you didn't bother to tell her," he had challenged her squarely but Georgie hadn't been able to come up with a ready answer. Maybe too intellectual a question? It was all he could do not to enquire if being an heiress had anything to do with it. He wondered how long Georgie would go on hiding that fact from herself? Inwardly disgusted, Cal made a swift charge up the few remaining stone steps, lifting a hand in greeting to another young cousin who beamed at him. Nice kid, Tim. He'd always enjoyed having him out to Jingala, the MacFarlane ancestral desert stronghold, for holidays.

"How's it going, Tim?"

"Great, just great, Cal," the young fellow responded, feeling mightily relieved to see his dynamic cousin who so emanated authority. "I was just about to ask this lady…"

Cal turned away from his hero worshipping young cousin to centre his gaze on the "loose cannon".

A voice in his head spoke as loud and clear as any oracle: *This, MacFarlane, is your kind of woman.*

The realisation made his whole body tense. Wouldn't that be one hell of a thing—to get involved with Ms Wyatt, a woman on the rebound? Yet he swore a leap of something extraordinary passed between them—something well outside an eroticized thrill. *Recognition?* Such things happened. Instantaneous connection? The wise man would do well to ignore the phenomenon. The wise woman too. The question remained. How in the world had Sinclair given up this goddess for Georgie, even if Georgie came draped in diamonds, rubies and pearls?

Cal held the goddess's gaze for long measuring seconds, more entranced than he cared to be. Even his cynical old heart seemed to have gone into temporary meltdown. He reined himself in. The sweetest woman could suck the life out of a man, as his bolter mother had sucked the life out of his dad.

"Sorry I'm late. I got held up by a phone call." He took her arm in a light grasp, disturbed to find she was trembling.

Yet she had the wit to reply smoothly, "No problem." If that weren't enough, she reached up and calmly kissed his cheek. "As you can see, I made it on my own."

"You look wonderful!" He didn't have to strain to say that.

"Thank you so much." She gave him a smile that would have taken most men's breath away.

Okay, so that smile affected him! Lucky for him he'd built up an immunity to beautiful women with smiles like the sunrise.

"So do you," she returned the compliment. "I've rarely seen a man wear a morning suit so well." She had no difficulty in acknowledging the simple truth. He was a very handsome man in a style that hitherto hadn't been her cup of tea. She went for a *gentler* look. If Sean's looks were often described as "boyish", this guy was *hard set handsome*, with electricity crackling all around him. Strong cleft chin. Very tall, very lean with a strongly built frame. Not *macho*. Nothing as self-conscious or as swaggering as that. Here was a guy who was strong in every sense of the word. Maybe too aggressively *male* for her taste. And how exactly was he eyeing her?

"Shall we go in?" Cal suggested smoothly. Obviously they couldn't go back down the steps. She had exquisite creamy skin and the nearest thing he'd seen to golden eyes. It was the oddest thing, but he wanted to sweep off that confounded hat so he could see her hair, which appeared to be a wonderful vibrant bright copper…no, amber, which no doubt accounted for her name.

"Just what I was thinking," she agreed in a sweetly accommodating voice.

It didn't fool him one bit. This was one beautiful woman laden with *intent*. She was here for one singular purpose. To create an almighty stir. So far she was doing extremely well. Little whispers were being passed from one wedding guest to another. There was a lot of compulsive head swivelling, short gasps. Some were staring openly, making no bones about their avid interest. Not that he altogether blamed her for doing this. It took a lot of nerve. But it was his job to stop her. It must have been appalling for Amber Wyatt, squarely in the public eye, to be so publicly humiliated. Sinclair must come from a long line of jackals.

"See you later on, Tim," he called to his young cousin, aware that Tim was looking after them in wonderment as he swept this gutsy, downright foolhardy young woman inside the church.

Who is he? Amber, despite appearances, was only just managing to keep her nerve. She had to admit this guy was something to behold—and chock-a-block with surprises. She had fully expected to be exposed as a woman in the commission of a serious crime, yet he was acting as though they were a couple. Did he feel desperately sorry for her? Or was he someone who would bundle her out of a side door after a few chastening words? It took her roughly ten seconds to hit on the last option. He wouldn't have much difficulty doing it. He was several inches over six feet and looked superbly fit. She could see the ripple of lean muscle beneath the close fit of his jacket. He was enormously self-assured. Probably had every reason to be. The unshakeable air of male supremacy that generally put her teeth on edge was well in evidence. It warned against any outrageous behaviour on her part. That and a certain glitter in his eyes. They were—well—*lovely*, though he would probably cringe to hear that. Shots of sparkling colour in his bronzed face—the cool green of one of her favourite gemstones, the peridot. She couldn't help registering that not only was the colour remarkable, so too was the intensity.

One thing was certain. She had never seen him before in her life. She'd remember. She liked the fact that she had to tilt her head to look up at him. Not something she did every day. Sean had been forever asking her to wear low heels or even flatties, when she was a girl for whom high heels were not only a necessity but a passion.

Now that her eyes had adjusted to the cool interior of the church after the brilliant sunshine outside, she could see that it was beautifully decorated. She bit down hard on her lip lest a cry escape her.

Even so, it did. "Aah!"

"You'll get through it," he told her, his expression Byronic.

"How did I ever convince myself I loved him? Why did I choose him of all the men in the world to marry?" she wailed.

"Seemed like a good idea at the time? You couldn't have been short of other offers."

"So what does that say about me? I'm a very poor judge of character?" Zara, unfairly regarded by some as an airhead, had seen through him right from the beginning.

"Maybe love—or what passes for it—truly is blind."

"It *wasn't* love." She shook her head. More being in love with love. The constant awareness that her biological clock was ticking away? She was twenty-six. She wanted kids. She loved children and they loved her. She had four godchildren at the last count. She was a real favourite with her friends. A marvellous, trustworthy babysitter.

Time to break off her philosophical meanderings with her new best friend.

Masses and masses of white and soft cream flowers shimmered before her distressed eyes. Roses, lilies, peonies, double cream lisianthus, carnations, gladiolus and the exquisitely delicate ivory-white petals of the Phalaenopsis orchids, all wonderfully and inventively arranged. And oh, the perfume! The rows of dark polished pews were lavishly beribboned in white and cream taffeta.

Amber just stood there, letting it all overwhelm her.

Her rescuer drew her to one side as the wedding guests continued to stream in. Amber watched dazedly as he acknowledged this one and that, giving what appeared to be a reassuring inclination of his head to a stony-faced society matron in a drop-dead ghastly misfit of a hat. If looks could annihilate, Amber was sure she would be gasping her last breath. But of course! It was the bride's mother. As such, didn't she have a right to demand Amber be thrown out? Mrs Rosemary Erskine in the flesh was an awesome sight.

It was all so unreal she might have been having an out of body experience. And who was this man who kept a light but *secure* rein on her? Obviously, he was well known. His thick crow-black hair, swept back from a high brow, had a decided deep wave that was clipped to control. The bronze of his skin wasn't fake. That tan came from a life in the sun. The light grey morning suit, which a lot of men couldn't successfully carry off, only served to accentuate his height, width of shoulder and the natural elegance of his body. A man of action? He wasn't any man about town. Impossible to remain anonymous when you looked like that. He certainly wasn't a friend of Sean's—his friends tended to be much like himself—so he had to be from the bride's side.

"Ms Wyatt, isn't it?" His voice, as classy as the rest of him, broke into her speculations.

"Round one to you. I can't for the life of me figure out who *you* are and I'm really trying." Though she spoke banteringly, she felt like a butterfly about to be pinned for his private collection. Indeed her heart was fluttering like a butterfly trapped in a cage. He had a beautiful mouth. How odd that she should even notice. Firm, very clean-cut, the rims slightly raised. He was someone Zee would describe as *drop dead sexy*. She was almost on the point of conceding that herself.

She wondered what he would look like when he smiled. Teeth were important to her. Good teeth. Even on this humiliating day, a woman publicly scorned, she couldn't seem to take her eyes off a perfect stranger. But then that was her training, she reassured herself. Her life as a journalist was spent checking people out, remembering faces. She was naturally observant.

"Cal MacFarlane," he introduced himself. "I'm the bride's cousin."

Her heart shook. But she wasn't ready to buckle. Instead, she levelled him with a dubious stare. "Really? You don't look in the least like her." He looked more like that British actor Clive Owen. The same uber-male aura.

"I'm a MacFarlane, but we do share a grandfather, Sir Clive Erskine."

"Ah, yes, Sir Clive." She nibbled on her lower lip as her memory bank opened up. "You're the Cattle Baron, right?" She was tuned in to a degree.

"Exactly." Amusement cut sexy little grooves into the corners of his mouth. "You're awfully audacious coming here, aren't you, Ms Wyatt?"

She decided to wing it. After all, he couldn't be one hundred per cent sure. "How do you know Sean didn't send me an invitation? We were very close up until *very* recently."

"So you intend to go out in a blaze of notoriety?" Her skewed gallantry smote his hard heart.

"Mr MacFarlane, I don't know what you mean." She let some of the sweetness slide. "I'm dedicated to doing the right thing. Or I have been up to date. And where did it get me? Lighten up. I promise I won't cause any *real* bother."

"You're causing it already," he told her very dryly. "This isn't a joyous occasion, is it? Not for you and not particularly for me. I think, ultimately, my cousin is going to have to pay for marrying Sinclair in more ways than one."

Amber's brows rose. "Sweet Lord!" she said reverently. "You've got Sean's measure already! It took me ages."

"How that must lacerate you."

"It does. I take it you don't like him either?"

He inched her further away from the front doors. "I only

met him last night. I fear he may be totally unscrupulous which is one reason why I'm standing here *with* you instead of ushering you out the back."

Her gaze turned appealing. "Come on, you wouldn't do that?"

"Not if we can work something out."

"Actually, I was hoping you wouldn't interfere."

"Haven't I just told you I'm family?" He smiled down into her face.

"Well, I don't need you to feel *sorry* for me." God, what a smile!

"I'm *not* sorry for you. I think you've had a lucky escape. So what are we going to do? Team decision. The bride will be arriving any minute."

"Why, take our seats, of course." She tried to peer around those wide shoulders.

"Tell you what, I'll sit beside you." Humour hovered around his mouth. "How's that?"

"But I wouldn't dream of taking you away from the bosom of your family Mr MacFarlane."

"No problem. On second thoughts, I think we might slip up to the choir loft." He cast a quick glance upwards. "We can't be standing here when Georgie and her entourage arrives. By the sound of the clapping outside, it's about to happen."

"I do love it when they clap," she said bleakly. "Supposing we stand here and goggle. After all, your cousin is the wittiest, prettiest, richest girl in town. And the most underhand. She stole my fiancé—such as he is—right from under my nose."

"And I understand your hurt. But my guess is you'll live to thank her. I suggest the choir loft. *Now*. Move it, Ms Wyatt. I'm quite capable of picking you up."

"What, and fling me over your shoulder?"

"If I have to." He slipped an arm around her waist and steered her towards the curving flight of wooden steps.

"I don't know that I *want* to." She was endeavouring to resist him but not making much headway.

"I don't care what you want. Just *do* it. Sinclair might *deserve* a bloody good fright but he's not worth it."

"Why don't *we* get married?" she turned her head over her shoulder to ask with biting sarcasm.

"Well, you were about to do a hell of a lot worse."

The organist and the well known lyric soprano who had been hired to sing a selection of the bride's favourite hymns looked around, startled, as they made their unexpected appearance in the spacious loft.

"Go ahead. Don't take any notice of us." Amber wiggled her fingers when she really wanted to scream. The cattle baron could ruin everything. "You have a lot to answer for, forcing me up here." She kept it to a mere whisper. His ears were set beautifully against his shapely head. Sean's weren't. That was why he always wore his hair full and floppy.

"You'll thank me in the end. Why don't we find somewhere safe and sit it out? Unless you really do want to see the bride arriving?"

"Don't you?" She was taken aback. "I mean, you're family."

"So I am," he reminded himself. "You look beautiful, by the way." As exquisite as a long-stemmed rose. "All things pass, Ms Wyatt. I'm merely preventing you from making a spectacle of yourself. You could lose your job, do you know that? My grandfather has influence everywhere. I believe he was impressed with the way you've handled yourself up to date. Don't give him cause to damage your career," Cal warned. "My grandfather can be ruthless when opposed or seriously displeased. In coming here today, you've run a big risk."

"Get a lawyer. Sue me." She broke off as the organist started up with a great ear-splitting fanfare that had her instinctively wrapping her ears with her hands. "God, that's worse than a car alarm," she muttered.

Even the cattle baron, used to stampedes, was looking aghast. "I'm tempted to go over to the balustrade and throw something." The organist, on a roll, belted out the triumphant opening bars of Mendelssohn's *Wedding March*. Why, oh why, did organists have to hit the keys so hard? Pianists didn't hit the keys like that, even at a double forte.

"One can only wonder how the soprano will compete when her time comes," Cal observed sardonically.

"How corny can you get? Mendelssohn!" Tears sprang into Amber's eyes.

"No time to cry," he warned her.

"Mr Tough Guy."

"No, I'm a softie at heart. And no point in taking it out on the composer. Poor old Mendelssohn had to work like everyone else."

"Except your cousin," she reminded him tightly. "She must have fallen through the cracks. So are you going to take a peek at what she looks like? The dress is said to have cost thousands and thousands. I've heard she's carrying a teeny bit of excess weight."

"And who knows how long her pre-wedding diet will last?" He glanced down at the jilted Ms Wyatt, seeing the combination of delicacy, strength and intelligence in her features. He also saw the tremendous upset. She was very lovely. Beauty could sometimes be severe. She was beautiful in a tender way. Not even an old cynic like him could view such a woman with indifference. "Now, don't go worrying about me. I've been to a thousand weddings." He took a firm hold of her hand, just in case she decided to storm the balustrade.

"Is that what made you determined to remain a bachelor? You *are*, aren't you? You don't look tamed at all." In fact he looked as *untamed* as a high coasting eagle.

"I'm comfortable with it," he told her smoothly. "If I didn't want children, I don't think I'd get married at all."

"Same with me. But don't you get lonely, way out there in the Never Never?"

"Don't have time to be lonely," he said.

"I spotted you right off for a hard-working man. Listen, I'm going to take a peek. No one would hear me if I yelled something impolite, with that bloody organ." She stood up and immediately he joined her.

"Promise you'll be good?"

"When *haven't* I been good?" she muttered bitterly.

"Just make sure you don't throw your hat."

"Would you blame me?"

"I prefer you keep it. I love it."

He gave her another one of his smiles. It had the most peculiar effect on her knees. And his teeth were *perfect*. Beautifully straight and white.

"Keep your chin up, Amber. I may call you Amber? You can't really love a man who crawled out from under a rock."

The bride wore white duchesse satin decorated with crystals, silver beads and thousands of seed pearls, hand-applied. The waist appeared narrow, so she had to be wearing a boned waist-cincher, which made her bosom flare out of the tight-fitting bodice. Her sheer organza veil, complete with long train, was held off her face by a diamond tiara that Amber considered pretentious. The wedding guests didn't. They responded with a spontaneous burst of applause that seemed to go on over-long, even for a billionaire's granddaughter. The bridesmaids—there were four—all taller and slimmer than the bride, wore strapless chiffon gowns in pastel colours with tiny flowers twisted into their faintly messy height-of-fashion hairdos. To add to the spectacle, there was an angelic little flower girl with golden curls carrying a basket brimming with rose petals that she was scattering about the aisle with joyful abandon. The women guests wearing high heels would have to be very careful when the time came for them to step back into the aisle or come a cropper.

"Where did she get the tiara?" Amber whispered. "Borrow it from the Queen?"

"The Queen doesn't give tiaras away, except to her own. Look, why don't you go and sit down? There's nothing here for you but heartache."

Wasn't that the truth?

CHAPTER TWO

THERE was a proud smile on Sean's face. He looked *happy*! Amber had a terrible image of him, cavorting naked on his wedding night, a glass of Bollinger in hand. Sean loved Bollinger. He also loved getting rid of his clothes. Amber forced herself not to make a sound, yet the Cattle Baron took her hand, his grip tight and reassuring. She rather liked the feel of those calluses. What might they be like on a woman's body? In a mystifying way, just having him there was like being wrapped in a security blanket.

Once during the ceremony she felt faint and he put his arm around her. He smelled *wonderful*! And he was being so kind when he didn't look particularly kind. He was a perfect stranger, yet somehow they had made a connection. Either that or he had reasoned that this was the best way to keep her quiet. She couldn't lose sight of the fact that his loyalty lay with his family. Still, he *was* being genuinely kind. Some things you couldn't fake.

How long was it going to go on? Quite a while more with the Bishop in the spotlight. A handsome man, he traded on the fact that he looked a bit like Prince Philip. She couldn't have borne a long Nuptial Mass. At least the soprano sang in tune, her high notes soaring above the hellish din of the organ. The organist kept moving about on the stool. Why? Had white ants taken up residence in it? What should the soprano break into, of all things, but that old war horse "O Promise Me?"

It was the blackest of black jokes.

When had Sean first started having sex with his little bride? Amber's mind was seized by that thought. When had he first realised the Erskine heiress was his for the taking? Not that Sean was all that terrific in bed, she found herself suddenly considering, though he had considered himself a real stud. She, on the other hand, had got around to thinking that great sex didn't have to mean everything. Well, not absolutely everything. Sean had been such fun—good company, charming, good-humoured, though he did tend to laugh a lot at his own jokes. Then he'd messed up by being miserably unfaithful. There had been a time when she had actually considered letting him move in with her. At least she had been spared that.

When the time came for him to make his vows he spoke in a calm, strong voice that resonated around the church. A born actor. The bride's responses were as soft and gentle as the cooing of doves. Totally dispirited, Amber slumped back against the Cattle Baron. He'd been great. Pity their paths would never, never cross again. The two of them were pressed together like co-conspirators or maybe, to the casual observer, lovers. She just bet if *this* guy committed to a woman he would never betray her.

The moment arrived. The Bishop began to ask that crucial question of the congregation. Surely none had the expectation of hearing a voice yell Stop! Amber felt her heart swell with anger. She had done the best she could all these past weeks. She had behaved impeccably, even when mikes had been thrust under her nose and cameras had gone off in her face, recording her instinctive flinch. She had even gone so far as to wish the couple well. But now? Didn't despicable behaviour count against anyone any more? Had they rewritten all the rules of common decency? It wasn't that long ago that she could have sued him for breach of promise. Surely some degree of payback was in order? Sean was lucky she was an upright citizen and not some member of a notorious crime family who boasted about giving people who offended them "cement shoes".

Cal, who had supported the goddess all this time—no hardship whatever—felt the moment of crisis when the adrenalin started to pump through her blood. Her willowy body stirred from near swooning into action. Ms Amber Wyatt was about to cause an upheaval. The question was, what did she intend to do? Her fiery expression indicated something spectacular. Something *hugely* embarrassing for all concerned and shockingly inadvisable for her. She could finish up waiting tables.

Sinclair and Georgie were as good as married. Nothing could stop that, but at least he could prevent Ms Wyatt from doing something she would live to regret.

"Come here." He pulled her urgently to him.

Completely off balance, Amber found herself doing exactly what she was told. He was that kind of man. She couldn't push him away. He was much too strong. She didn't even know if she *wanted* to. This was the most extraordinary pseudo-embrace she had experienced in her life.

He literally crushed her to him.

God, a *real* man! She had a crazy notion of being ravished. Quite possibly she'd let him. If not now, at the first opportunity. Even as her mind spun out of control, he propelled her back across the loft, then, before she could recover, lowered his head and kissed her in a way that she knew with absolute certainty would leave a lasting memory. She even regressed to her teens…all those fabulous bodice-rippers she had devoured.

Her body felt sparkly all over, trembling under the influence of a battery of energising electric shocks. The pressure of that firm mouth coming down over hers, the sheer heart stopping eroticism, had her opening her soft lips like a rose opened up its petals to be drenched by the sun. The pleasure was tremendous.

Should she be craving such pleasure *now*? It was bizarre! It made a mockery of her engagement to Sean. This man's tongue was locating erogenous zones inside her mouth that had her seizing his lapels. What in the world had taken possession of her? Maybe she was getting the pain and humiliation out of her system? More likely it was the sheer *power* of this man, the way he handled himself. Even as she clutched him, he moved her closer in.

She was receiving the full impact of his superb male body. A natural scent came off his skin—warm fine leather, sunshine, the great outdoors, just the right touch of aftershave. Both of them were behaving like lovers in the white-hot grip of passion. She had no history of such extravagant behaviour.

Did *he*?

One didn't associate this unbridled behaviour with perfect strangers. It had to be something else. Both of them were playing a role. That was it! Playing it to the hilt! Either that or she had morphed into an entirely different person. Only as recent as five minutes ago, she had thought herself desperately unhappy. Now, heat was spreading through her body, into her stomach, plunging lower…

Oh, Amber, Amber, have a care!

Could shock and unhappiness derange a woman's body as well as her brain? Did being jilted loosen a girl's morals? Or was this a temporary state of dementia?

Whatever it was, the incandescent *glow* behind her eyes remained even when she was able to lift her heavy lids. She had never felt such sexual excitement with Sean. Now this tumultuous reaction with a *kiss*! Had it something to do with the dominant male? Had Sean been a subordinate male? She would have to give that a lot of thought. But it would have to be later on, when she was safely on her own.

"Well, it didn't take us long to make friends," he remarked with breathtaking coolness.

The tricky part was to find her voice. "Is that what it was? I thought it was more a spur of the moment bid to shut me up."

"And there's no doubt it worked! Further, Ms Wyatt, it was an absolute pleasure."

"You could have shown a bit more restraint." She put a trembling hand to her mussed hair.

"Don't be picky. *You* were going for broke. Anyway, don't let's worry about it. Look, your beautiful hat has floated off." It was now wedged in a cool dark corner, the petals of the pink and cream silk roses softly gleaming. He moved in what seemed like slow motion to pick it up, brushing off a speck of dust before restoring it to her. Amber, never short of a word, couldn't even utter *thank you*. Her heart was pounding hard and fast. Her legs were weak. Had there been a smoke alarm in the loft, she was sure it would have gone off. What did it all mean?

Cal found himself stretching out a hand to smooth her glowing hair. It was in disarray and such an indescribable shade! Tone on tone, from golden through to dark copper with glossy strands of apricot and Titian woven through. She wore it pulled back into a lustrous updated chignon—appropriate, he supposed, when wearing a picture hat like that.

"Look, I'm sorry," he said, when he clearly wasn't. "But it seemed like a good idea at the time. I *had* to stop you. Whatever you had in mind, you would only have regretted later."

"Is that an apology?"

"Could be." His laugh was slightly off-key. "Maybe we can discuss it more fully over dinner?"

She drew back, astonished . "Wh-a-a-t?"

"Not a trick question. Let me break it down. Are—you—free—for—dinner?"

"Are you serious?" Her beautiful golden eyes grew huge.

"Of course I am." He smiled at her confusion. "We can relax now. It's all over."

"So it is." Amber exhaled a deep sigh. "So what do we do now?"

"Well, I'm up for anything," he mocked. "We could continue kissing until you can't remember you ever had a fiancé?"

"Who is now married to your cousin. Thank you, but no, Mr MacFarlane. I don't think you could top the first kiss anyway."

"Well, I'd like to give it a shot," he returned smoothly. "You're not *still* looking for a husband, are you?"

She met the sparkling ironic gaze that was fairly centred on her. "I could very well remain married to a career. I may have climbed the ladder in television, but actually I want to be a writer. You know, another Colleen McCullough. *Love* her."

"Another *Thorn Birds*?"

"I wish! But I *can* write."

"You might have to make a start after today," he suggested dryly. He may have prevented Ms Wyatt from causing further disturbance and bringing down the full force of Rosemary's wrath on her beautiful head, but a lot of people had marked her imprudent attendance. Cal had a hollow feeling that there could be unpleasant repercussions for Ms Amber Wyatt. They were a vengeful lot, the Erskines.

"Is that a warning?"

"I'm putting you on your guard." He looked serious.

"I see. Your dear aunt was giving me the evil eye."

"Aunt by marriage," he corrected.

"Well, she does lack your style. I take it one wouldn't want to cross her."

"Believe me, when Rosemary is crossed, heads roll."

"That's the downside of having too much money," Amber murmured caustically. "I can't imagine her getting the better of you."

"Well, I do have the advantage of living well over a thousand miles away. But don't worry, Ms Wyatt, I'm going to put in a good word for you."

"*Why*, exactly?" She stared up at him. It was, she found, a very pleasant sensation. He made her feel almost petite.

"I was engaged once," he remarked, offhandedly. "I didn't exactly catch my fiancée in the arms of her stop-gap lover, but a good friend of mine happened to bump into them when they were taking a little holiday together in Bangkok. That's classified information, by the way."

"My lips are sealed." Amber made a little sealing gesture with her pearl-tipped fingers, astonished by his admission. "How could she possibly have preferred the other guy to *you*?"

His laugh was off-key. "Thanks for that little vote of confidence, Ms Wyatt. You would have to understand my ex-fiancée. Sexual encounters on the side she didn't regard as *meaningful*."

"But it was the end of the engagement for you?"

"Most definitely, though she tells it differently. That, again, is between the two of us, okay?"

She nodded. "Mr MacFarlane, I am to be trusted. Besides, I owe you one. So what now?"

He looked down into the fast emptying church. "You stay here until the church clears. I have to join the family—stick around until the happy couple embark on their wedded bliss."

"They've already done that," Amber said tartly. "Don't be surprised if Sean takes it into his head to run off with one of the bridesmaids." She settled her lovely picture hat back on her head, looking at him to check the angle. "Have I got it right?"

"Perfect! No woman could look more ravishing. Now, you can follow when the coast is clear. Everyone will be focused on getting to the reception. You should be able to make your escape."

"I didn't come here to make a spectacle of myself, you know." Suddenly she wanted to explain herself to him. She didn't want him to think badly of her. "Or disrupt the service, as you seemed to think. Sean really deserved it, but that wasn't my intention. That would have been cruel and I'm not a cruel person. The plan was to calmly walk out when the Bishop called for any objections—you know the bit—but I just felt so *angry* I momentarily lost control."

"You're free of him now."

"So I am." She couldn't conceal the bitterness and the pain.

"So what about dinner?" He repeated the invitation bracingly, as if dinner would be a form of therapy. "Are you up for it? I think it might do you a lot of good to be seen out on the town enjoying yourself. Or making a good show of it."

She felt a moment of turmoil, not knowing if it was a good or a bad thing. Was it possible she was getting into very deep water? Being with Sean, it had only come up to her ankles, she now realised. "Why are you being so kind?"

"I'm not being kind. Not at all." He cast a quick look at the near-empty pews. "I just don't feel ready to say goodbye to you, Ms Wyatt. That's all. I fly home in a few days."

"In your own little Airbus?" She lifted her high arching brows. "It's so nice to be rich."

"I assure you it's quite an effort holding on to it. However, where I come from, having your own plane is a necessity, not a rich man's toy. I have a couple of helicopters as well."

"I'm terrified of those," she said. "I was involved in a scare in the TV station's chopper some months ago. Anyway, aren't you supposed to be attending the reception? It will go on for hours and hours."

"Not for me it won't," he said firmly. "Where do you live?"

She held up her hands. "Please…no. This is madness!" She wasn't at all sure she could handle a man like this. Sean had been one thing. This man was really, *really* something else.

"Maybe that's why I like it." He smiled. "Address, please?" He checked again on the remaining number of guests. Maybe a dozen. The organist was still playing triumphantly, although the soprano, probably with perforated eardrums, had made her escape.

"I don't know if this is a good idea." Amber, who never dithered, dithered. How could a woman feel like jumping off a cliff one minute and be going out to dinner with a handsome stranger the next? But then she realized that it *did* happen.

"Just give me your address," he prompted.

Bemusedly, she did so. She might need him to put in a good word for her with his Godzilla of an aunt by marriage.

"I'll pick you up at nine," he informed her briskly. "I'll be able to make it by then. You'll feel better if you're out and about."

"Just don't alert the paparazzi."

He laughed, lifted a hand in salute, then began moving lithely down the flight of stairs.

His grandfather, accompanied by Rosemary, lost no time in seeking him out. They looked an incongruous duo, propelling their way towards him like two ocean-going liners breasting the high seas. Rosemary was a big woman who had become ever more substantial over the years. She towered over her father-in-law. But whereas Rosemary had reduced her doomed husband, Ian, to a tiny planet in orbit around her, his formidable grandfather radiated power, authority and a kind of physical indestructibility.

It had always been like that. Cal's mother, the bolter, Stephanie, was Sir Clive's only daughter. Her brother, Ian, was Georgie's father, the only son. Their mother, Rochelle, had been killed a week after her fortieth birthday when her high-powered sports car, a birthday present, had slammed into a brick wall, doing one hundred miles per hour. Ian had taken after his father in looks if nothing else; Stephanie had inherited Rochelle's beauty, wit and high octane nature. Stephanie had been idolized by Sir Clive and endlessly indulged, whereas Ian had never been able to cope with a stern and exacting father's expectations and demands.

Georgie, the Erskine heiress, had never worked a day in her life. But then she hadn't lived a life devoted exclusively to the pursuit of pleasure either. Georgie, like her father, lived her life under Rosemary's thumb. How then had a moral lightweight like Sinclair hoodwinked Rosemary, let alone his grandfather, into thinking he would make Georgie a good husband? Cal had believed them more than capable of sniffing out a rat. Well, they would know soon enough. Ms Amber Wyatt had made a very lucky escape. He didn't doubt that for a minute.

His grandfather laid a steely hand on his arm. "I want to thank you, Cal, for getting that outrageous young woman out of harm's way. What was she thinking of, coming to the church? Simply not done!" he huffed. "Especially not to me or my family. She'd behaved herself up until now. I had every intention of offering her a holiday. Anywhere in the world she cared to go. Certainly not now. That's gone by the board." He nodded his large balding head several times, then pulled his right ear lobe.

"Why not forget it?" Cal suggested. "Maybe she shouldn't have turned out for the wedding, but she must have taken the public humiliation hard. A lot of women in her shoes might have been prepared to do a whole lot worse."

"That was bad enough," Sir Clive grunted, still red in the face. "You're not defending her, surely, m'boy?"

"I suppose I am," Cal admitted. He was in no way intimidated by his authoritarian maternal grandfather. Not even as a child.

"I can't believe this!" Rosemary shook with rage. "Seeing that girl arrive was almost the death of me. To think she would try to spoil our Georgie's big day!"

"It could have been a lot worse," Cal said provocatively. "As I understand it, Ms Wyatt has drawn a lot of public sympathy."

"Cheap! She's cheap, cheap, cheap!" Rosemary glared back, shoulders shuddering. "Of course she's very beautiful."

"Dangerously so," he suavely agreed. "But she didn't intend to do anything too dreadful."

"That's your view, is it?" Sir Clive gave a sudden bark. He stared back at Cal as if he had suddenly gone mad. Worse—disloyal. "This was your cousin's—*my* granddaughter's—big day, might I remind you, Cal? A bloody fortune has gone into it." Even he had been gobsmacked by the cost.

"You know it was well worth it, Grandfather, dear," Rosemary appealed to her father-in-law, who had fronted the monumental bill.

That didn't curb Sir Clive's rage. "That young lady made one very big mistake today. It has turned me against her. The whole thing will be reported in the newspapers. I don't take kindly to being made a fool of. What exactly did she intend to do?"

"Nothing really. She just took it into her head to attend."

"You're covering for her, Callum," Rosemary said with fierce disapproval. "There's only one explanation—she intended to cause a massive scene. You couldn't let her do that."

"No, of course I couldn't," Cal agreed quietly; he had known Ms Amber Wyatt was a bundle of trouble from the moment he had laid eyes on her. "But I'm defending her because she came quietly. Always a good sign. If she were as bad as you seem to think, she could have turned on quite a show. Instead, she let me escort her up to the organ loft."

Rosemary showed her mean eyes. "I think it had more to do with the fact she knew she wasn't any match for you. All through the ceremony my Georgie would have been frantic with worry. Sean too. Which brings me to why he said he had to be free of her."

Cal kept his eyes fixed on Rosemary's face. "Do tell, Rosemary. You're dying to. Why did your son-in-law have to make the break? A physical description of Ms Wyatt would have to be glorious."

"Be careful you're not giving yourself away, Callum,"

Rosemary retaliated, nostrils flaring. "You always were susceptible to a beautiful woman. Take Brooke now—"

"That will do, Rosemary," Sir Clive sternly intervened. "Kindly remember this is my grandson you're talking to. Brooke Rowlands wasn't anywhere near good enough for Callum. Now, we have to go in to our guests. This is supposed to be a joyous occasion. I have to tell you I'm none too happy about Georgie's new husband, but the deed is done. We would have had to admit her to a psychiatric facility if any of us had tried to stop her. That doesn't excuse Ms Wyatt's part in the day's proceedings, however. She looks such a lady too. I'm disappointed. However, for this outrage she might find herself behind the cameras for a while. Give her time to reflect."

It was as good as done, Cal thought. His grandfather was way too powerful.

CHAPTER THREE

AMBER had only been inside her apartment six or seven minutes when Jono knocked on the door, his mobile face bright with anticipation.

"Well, how did it go?"

Amber stood back, waving him in. "It was very, very sad."

"Really?" Jono spun. "What happened? Remember you can't keep it private, sweetie."

Amber led him into the stylishly decorated living room. "Like a coffee or something?"

"Let me make it. You just sit down and talk to me. You don't *look* sad."

"Oh, how do I look?" She was quite unaware that she looked radiant from head to toe.

"Like you've just met some new guy, hot on the heels of the old?"

"What makes you think I *want* a new guy?"

"You mightn't think so now, dear, but you will," Jono told her with certainty. "When that dirty rotten scoundrel Sean committed to being a love rat he made up his mind to be the best one around. But there *are* good men out there, Amby. Never doubt it. Sometimes I wish I weren't gay."

"Don't tell Jett that." She had to smile. She did a lot of smiling when Jono and his partner, Jett, a fellow computer whiz, were around. "But there *was* a new guy. The bride's cousin, of all things. He was the one who dealt with me."

"Lord sakes! He didn't chuck you out?" Jono paused in what he was doing.

"No. He whisked me off to the organ loft and stayed with me throughout. He's a Cattle Baron by name of Cal MacFarlane."

"A Cattle Baron!" Jono shrieked, throwing up his hands. "Not a redneck, I hope?" He set the coffee to perk. "Rich?"

"Without a doubt. And he's no redneck. He's very cultured. His grandpop is Sir Clive Erskine."

Jono's face fell. "Then he *can't* be good-looking. There's always a downside."

"Oh, I don't know. How does Clive Owen-ish sound?"

Jono's jaw dropped. "You're joking."

"You can meet him if you like," Amber promised. "He's picking me up at nine. We're going out to dinner."

Jono whistled in admiration. "And I thought I was a fast worker! As I'm very fond of saying, love, life's an adventure. One chapter finishes, another begins."

The Cattle Baron had a limousine waiting. "You look ravishing."

Hugely gratified, she could see that he meant it. She had picked out a short, glittery gold dress that showed off her long limbs and, if she said it herself, a tantalizing décolletage.

"Thank you. Hard to get away?" He was still wearing his formal wedding suit. It was absurd how well it suited him.

"It wasn't *that* easy. But I'm here."

"So, what you promise you deliver?"

"I really do like it that way."

The uniformed chauffeur held the door while Amber slipped gracefully into the back seat. A moment more and the Cattle Baron joined her. She was almost shivery with the intimacy. He was just so *physical*, the quintessential man of action.

"So Jono and Jett are your friends?" he asked when they were underway.

"Jono for years now. He's a very clever, very gentle man. He likes to keep an eye out for me."

"You must feel good about that. He couldn't have approved of you know who."

"I don't have a clue who you're talking about," she said airily, gazing out of the window at the glittering cityscape, above it a starry sky.

"Right. I admire the way you've disposed of *that* problem."

"Where are we going, by the way?"

"The best establishment in town. Where else?"

Where else, indeed? It dawned on her that she was looking forward to spending a few hours with the Cattle Baron. In fact, she was excited. Didn't that underscore her poor judgement about Sean?

The restaurant was seriously good. Wonderful ambience, excellent, discreet service. She had dined there a number of times. Always as a guest, not the one footing the bill. No one in their right mind could say the price was right. But the food—inspirational stuff—was superb, the wine list a long selection of the very best the world's top vintners could offer, the upper end pricey enough to give even the well-off a heart attack.

"Tell me what wine you like?" the Cattle Baron asked, looking across a table set for two. One of the best positions in the room. How had he managed it on a Saturday night?

"And put you at my mercy?" she joked. "You've seen the prices."

"We can forget the prices for tonight," he told her calmly. "What if we start with a nice glass of champagne? Can't go past Krug. You have to celebrate your lucky escape." His cool green eyes glittered.

"Let me make it perfectly clear that I'm still upset."

"Of course you are. But the Krug will help."

It was all *too* tempting.

She had thought she never would again, but she laughed. Really laughed. She hadn't expected him to be so entertaining, but he was a born raconteur. He kept telling her wonderful stories about Outback life—hilarious incidents, interposed with the tragic and poignant realities of life in a harsh, unforgiving land. It was what gave him the heroic image, she suddenly realised. It was emblazoned all over him. *Hero figure.*

From the arrival of the *amuse bouches*, tempting little morsels to tease the palate, the starters, a carpaccio of tuna and swordfish garnished with a delicious little mix of green herbs, the main course of fillet of barramundi with a sweet-and-sour pepper sauce over risotto, the rim of the plate decorated with baby vegetables, he kept her enthralled. So much so she was eating with abandon. It struck her that they liked the same food, because independently they came up with the same choices. Even to the bitter chocolate mousse with coffee granita and gingered cream.

"That was superb," he said, laying down his dessert spoon.

"I know it. Good thing you're paying. There's a poor soul over there choking over the bill."

He laughed. "I daresay it takes a lot to run a three star restaurant and make a nice profit. Coffee?"

"Absolutely. I need to sober up."

"You won't be wanting a liqueur, then?" There was a twinkle in those mesmerizing green eyes.

"I didn't say that."

"So, feel ready to tell me a little about you," he said, settling back to enjoy his coffee.

"I knew there was a catch."

He leaned forward slightly, aware that they had been under

scrutiny since they had walked into the restaurant. She was obviously well known. He wasn't. But he *was* wearing wedding gear. A big clue. "I didn't ask if I could sleep at your place."

"Where *are* you staying?' She circled the rim of her coffee cup with a forefinger, not daring to look up and perhaps give her living dangerously self away.

"Why, with Grandpop, of course."

"He *does* have a mausoleum."

"And he insisted I stay over. I know it's not a nice thing to say, but I do my level best to avoid Rosemary."

"Look, I don't blame you. As soon as I got home I had to lie down to recover from her evil eye. So, your uncle and aunt and dear little Georgie—up until her dicey marriage—live with Grandpop?"

"You've got it."

Those distracting little sexy brackets at his mouth again. "So it's more than likely Georgie and Sean will move into the mausoleum when they return from Europe?" She was able to raise a blasé brow.

"I wouldn't be a bit surprised. It's a 'till death us do part' situation with Georgie and her mother."

"Poor thing! Even I can feel sorry for her. But not for Sean. How did he pass muster with your people anyway? Your grandfather is rumoured to have the hardest nut in town. Rosemary could have been a pushover. Sean can be very good at buttering up the women." Even a Brunhilde.

"Forget them," he said. "It's *you* I want to hear about. From the beginning. You must have been an extraordinarily pretty baby."

"My dad thought so." She couldn't stop a tender smile breaking out when tears still ran down the walls of her heart. "It was he who named me Amber. My mother wanted to call me Samantha."

"Then you'd have got Sam for short."

"So you think he made a better choice?"

"Amber suits you." His eyes were very bright. "You're an only child?"

"Yes."

"And your parents?"

She sighed deeply. "I lost my dad when I was fourteen. A teenage driver ran the red light and collected him in a crossing. He could have saved himself but he chose to save a child instead. A little boy and his mother were on the crossing at the same time. There could have been more people hurt.'

"I'm so sorry, Amber." He reached over to grip her hand, divining her sense of loss. "It's brutal losing a much loved parent."

"It is that." Her topaz eyes misted with tears. "My mother remarried the year I finished school. Needless to say, I didn't take to my new stepfather, though he's not a bad guy. Not my dad, though. I lived on campus through my university days. Not much to tell about the rest. I became a cadet journalist. Got a break on television. I guess the way I look has kept me there."

"You're being hard on yourself. Didn't you win a prestigious award for your article about street kids? It couldn't have been easy going into tough places. Exploring the drug scene, the Dead On Arrivals presenting at hospital, the hopelessness and deep depression."

"What do you think?" Unshed tears continued to shimmer in her eyes. "Some are born to sweet delight, some are born to endless night."

He nodded. 'You're still in touch with your mother?"

"Of course. I love my mother. But I don't see her as much as I'd like. They live in Cairns. They love the tropics, close to the Reef. My stepdad has money and a big motor cruiser. They take lots of trips because he's retired. Tell me about you."

"Me?" His mouth faintly twisted.

"Yes, you. You sound like you know all about missing a parent."

"It happens I do. Like you, I lost my dad, a little over four years ago. He ignored a gash in his arm until it was too late. Lots of barbed wire around the station. Died of septicaemia in a very short time."

"How terrible!" Amber felt moved to exclaim. "Couldn't your mother have made him see a doctor? Men can be so careless with their injuries."

"He'd had his shots. We all have them but the effects must have worn off. My mother left us for a guy I called Uncle Jeff for years of my childhood. So, no mother, no guardian angel. I was away at a trade conference when it happened."

"So you know all about having a hard time?"

"I learned. I grew tough."

"Well, you may *appear* tough—"

"Do I?" His look was very direct.

"In a striking sort of way. But you have a heart of gold. You've been very kind to me."

"What's kind about taking a beautiful woman out to dinner?" he asked, then issued a quiet warning. "Don't look up. The people at the table over there haven't taken their eyes off us since we walked in."

"Isn't that our cue to walk out?" she whispered back. They were finished anyway. The hours had rippled by like silk.

"Sure. What I really want to do is get a better look at your apartment."

"You sound hopeful."

His green eyes were amused. "I am."

"And then seduce me?"

He gave her that dizzying smile. "Ms Wyatt, if you knew how I *want* to! But I won't. Scout's honour. I really liked your apartment. You've got great taste. Besides, the night is young."

He turned his handsome raven head. "I wonder if they have a back door. I wouldn't be in the least surprised if there were photographers waiting for us out there. Someone is bound to have tipped them off."

Anyone would have thought she was a rock star. Even a TV star, albeit not in the ascendant wasn't safe anywhere. The paparazzi, as he'd predicted, *were* waiting.

"What do we do? Make a run for it?" She pushed herself into the sheltering crook of his arm. It was *so-o* good to have a man around. Especially one so big and strong. The limo wasn't too far off. He had instructed the chauffeur to meet them in the alleyway at the rear of the restaurant, where the more enterprising had gathered.

"Might as well let them get a few shots. But don't say a word," he advised.

"You got it, boss!" He was perfect in the role.

Afterwards, she thought she would be forever astonished by the speed and efficiency with which he shielded her from the mob, successfully steered her past all their shouted questions, then smoothly bundled her into the waiting limo. Even so, they got their shots. No matter! Wasn't that the reason she and the Cattle Baron had decided on a night on the town? She had proven beyond any doubt that she wasn't the girl to run and hide.

True to his word, he was the perfect gentleman. Clearly, he was a man to be trusted. She watched him roam her spacious living room, studying the artwork. Downlighters picked out the colours and brought the paintings to life, especially the large oil of a field of yellow tulips.

"That's good enough to step in and pick a bunch," he commented, thinking she had an excellent eye and a fine sense of style. She would love the paintings at Jingala. "Yellow would be your favourite colour, right?"

"How did you know?"

He took in a sharp breath. He had spent so much time turning his feelings into a fortress it was unnerving to know the whole damned apparatus could crumble into dust. Roaming about, he paused at her prize piece of sculpture, a large gilded bronze horse. As someone who was practically born in the saddle, he found the anatomy of the horse, the sense of movement, spot on.

"It cost me six months' salary and then some but it was worth it," she said.

"If you ever want to sell it, you have a buyer."

She shook her head.

"You ride?" He shot her a quick enquiring look. The downlights were caught in her glorious hair, which was brushed back from her smooth wide forehead and cascading loose.

Amber nodded. "I love horses. I belonged to a pony club as a child. My dad bought me my first pony when I was six."

"I bet he was so proud of you."

She bit her lip. "My dad thought I was a star. His shining star."

"I'm not surprised," he said very gently. "Have you been able to keep your riding up?" He picked up a jade snuff bottle, one of a small collection, examined it, then put it down again. "Nineteenth century?"

"Yes. Bought them in Hong Kong. I don't keep up my riding as much as I'd like. I don't—*didn't*—have a lot of free time. But nothing would stop me getting out now and then."

"Good!" He clipped it off as though he would have held it against her had she not tried.

The lush plants on her balcony too found favour—the luxuriant mass of philodendrons, large succulents and a variety of other plants. Later, he came to sit opposite her on one of her new sofas—soft, supple leather in an inviting shade of vanilla. One long arm shifted two of the silk cushions to one side. She hadn't the slightest desire to send him on his way. Instead, they fell back effortlessly into conversation…

It was all pretty astonishing stuff.

She had fully expected to cry herself to sleep that night. Instead, she found herself confiding to the Cattle Baron things she had never told anyone before.

Ships that pass in the night? That theory had been advanced.

He, in turn, didn't appear to hesitate in filling her in on his own life. Like her, he was an only child. He rarely saw his mother. He said it without visible upset or apology. Clearly, he had never forgiven her for deserting him and his father. More so for his father's sake, she thought. He spoke so glowingly of his father. It must have been a great relationship. That she could well understand. "I want him back," he said.

"Me, too. I want *my* dad back."

He had an uncle Eliot, his father's much younger brother, a mid-life child who lived with him on the MacFarlane cattle station. She made a mental note to learn more about Jingala, a historic station, she seemed to remember.

"Eliot lost his first wife, Caro, to breast cancer. It hit us all very hard. Caro was a lovely person, incredibly brave. And such a fighter. She should have won. We were afraid Eliot might do something…" He hesitated, his expression grim.

"Might harm himself," she gently supplied.

"You read that right. Janis came along almost two years ago. She's a few years older than I am. She's very good-looking in a high-strung sort of way. Jan got pregnant almost at once. They have a baby boy, Marcus, named after my father. My dad and Eliot were very close, more like father and son than brothers. The age difference and the fact that my father was the strong one, the stuff of legend. I love my uncle but he certainly has his problems."

"They weren't straightened out with his new wife and the

baby?" she asked. "I would have thought he'd be just so proud and happy."

"Well, of course he is proud and happy," he returned a shade tersely. "None of us thought he would ever remarry."

"What's worrying you?" she asked, studying his frowning face. Gosh, he was a handsome man! The more she looked at him, the more she was coming to develop a taste for the hard-wired dynamic male.

"Do I look worried?"

"It wasn't a match made in heaven?" she suggested soothingly.

His expression turned ironic. "Aren't matches made in heaven said to be like ghosts? One hears about them but never sees them. Jan is having a lot of difficulty bonding with little Marc."

"Well, now, that's *sad*." She was taken aback. "It's possible she's suffering post-natal depression. It's not at all uncommon, but it can't be allowed to go untreated. There *is* help."

He pushed an impatient hand through his thick dark hair, tousling the crisp waves. He should leave it like that, she thought. It looked great. "You don't think we've had it? The problem is that Jan rejects help. Anyway, I've said enough about that."

"But isn't there someone to persuade her—her own mother, a close friend? Surely they'd want to help?" It seemed very much as if her husband couldn't. Neither could the Cattle Baron, but it was obvious that he didn't want to interfere in his uncle's marriage.

"Jan and her mother aren't close," he said. "I think she stopped talking to her mother years ago. At any rate, she wasn't invited to the wedding. Another problematic family. Jan's mother and father divorced when she was around ten. Marriage break-ups always have repercussions."

She took a deep breath. "And you're not looking for a wife? Don't let—Brooke, wasn't it—sideline you."

"Don't let Sean sideline *you*," he retorted very smartly indeed.

"Well, both of us have jobs to do."

"I can only hope you have yours on Monday," he said. "Offending my grandfather is to encourage disaster."

"If the worse comes to the worst I guess I'll have to live with it," she said.

CHAPTER FOUR

THERE was a great shot of them in the Sunday papers: *Amber Wyatt and her Mystery Man*. They looked like a pair of movie stars. Anything to keep the public on the edge of their seats.

Monday morning came and she found to her horror that the Cattle Baron had been right. She didn't have a job any longer.

"What possessed you, Amber?" Paddy Sweeney, the station manager, asked in dismay. "You've really blown it *this* time, girl. Insulting old man Erskine! How bright is that? I'm worried about you. The public love you. The station would have tolerated just about anything from you, including appearing topless, but I have to tell you no one ticks off Clive Erskine. You did it Big Time. It doesn't make me happy—far from it—"

"Who likes to be the hatchet man?" She gave him a wry smile.

"Don't say that, love. You know how I've always fostered your career, but the order has come down from on high."

"The Almighty?" Anger was expressed in derision.

Paddy grunted. "Always supposin' the Big Fella exists. Or, to His everlasting credit, He doesn't like to interfere."

"Perish the thought! So, no warnings, no last chances, no last-minute reprieves?"

"I wish!" Paddy groaned. "It's such a shame. We're top of

the ratings. But it was a horrendous idea, showing up at the wedding, Amber. Why didn't you speak to me about it?"

"Hello, Paddy? I *did*."

He paled. "But I thought you were joking! You're always joking."

"You're kidding me."

"Amber, I'm sorry. To think I could have stopped you from causing a scandal"

"Oh, yeah?" Amber was getting angrier by the moment. It went with the red hair. "It was Mr and Mrs Sean Sinclair who caused the scandal," she snapped back. "Don't call *my* behaviour brazen, Paddy."

It was barely ten o'clock but Paddy looked as if he'd had a really rough day. "Amber, I know exactly what they put you through." He crunched up a memo and lobbed it at a waste paper basket. Missed. He always did. "Sinclair's a blaggard."

"No argument here. The thing is, he is now Sir Clive Erskine's grandson-in-law."

Paddy responded with a despondent wave of his hand. "You could have got away with most anything. But not this. Not for a good while, anyway. Even your chances of getting in to another channel are zero. No one will dare touch you. You crossed a very powerful man. Woe to the station who tries to pick you up. The old bugger would buy it just to make sure he got his way."

"So he's only posing as a pillar of the church?"

Paddy gave a sardonic laugh. "It's the way things work, Amber. Billionaires don't have to throw their weight around. They just give the order. People like Erskine are too powerful to fight."

"So I'm bounced for a misdemeanour?" Amber was trying hard to adjust to it.

"Erskine considers it a near crime. You got yourself engaged to a cad. He betrayed you. You're better off without him. He was never good enough for you."

"So I clear my desk? I take it I'm off air tonight?"

Paddy's cheeks turned ruddy. "I'm sorry, Amber. Really, really sorry. We all are."

"Not dear old Jack, I bet! Jack will be delighted to have the news slot to himself."

Paddy nodded his assent. "Only redeeming feature, he's a pro. He never stuffs up and he's got a great speaking voice."

"I prefer mine."

She stood up and Paddy stood too, coming around his desk to her. "Take a holiday," he advised.

"I'm thinking space travel."

"Keep that for a future project. Let things cool down. This isn't going to last for ever, love. The public will want to know where you are."

She gave a snort of disgust. "I bet it's all over town as we speak."

"And you can bet your life the whole country will be taking sides. Lie low, that's my advice. You know you've got a champion in me."

She gave him a forgiving smile. Paddy had to obey directives like everyone else. "Thanks for trying. You've been a great boss."

"Lemme work on it." Paddy escorted her to the door, genuinely upset. Taking Amber Wyatt off air just went to prove that no one, however popular, was indispensable. It was a tough game.

Stepping out of the lift as Amber was stepping in was the man himself, Jack Matthews.

"Hi, there, if it isn't the beauteous Ms Wyatt!" He greeted her with his trademark toothy smile. "Getting your sorry little ass out of here?"

No point in losing it. "No sound as sweet as your own voice, Jack."

"Good luck, anyway." He sketched a sardonic salute as the lift doors began to close. "You've no future in the television industry."

"Good to have an unbiased opinion, Jack."

There was something deeply satisfying about getting the last word.

Except that didn't happen.

"I'll miss you," Jack called.

Hang tough!

She was barely back in the apartment when someone pressed her door buzzer hard. Australia Post? Flowers and a sympathy card signed by the entire Channel? Maybe a get-out-of-town type delivery, hopefully not one that exploded. She checked the image that came up on the tiny video screen. Good heavens! The Cattle Baron. Erskine's grandson. Never forget that vital point.

"Didn't we agree you'd stop following me?" she said into the receiver.

"I'm *not* following you.'

Even over the crackle, he sounded good. "Never thought to phone ahead?"

"Took a chance with the visit. I'm here with a plan."

She rubbed her aching forehead. "Few things more unworkable than a plan, Mr MacFarlane. Please go away."

"You don't need help?" It was a challenge.

Common sense came to the rescue. "Lucky for you, I need all the help available. Does this plan involve travel?"

"How did you guess?"

"So long as it's not outer Mongolia." She released the security door. This guy had mesmerized her. The way he kissed. The way he talked. The way he looked. One hundred different warring sensations were assailing her all at once.

His sheer *physicality* was nigh on overwhelming within the

confines of her small entrance hall. He was wearing a crisp blue and white checked shirt in fine cotton, great-fitting jeans, a beige linen bomber jacket over the top. He could have posed for an ad for Calvin Klein. "You've got ten minutes. The clock's ticking. I take it you know I've been shunted?"

"The news was broken to me. Rather roughly, as it happens. I did warn you. Dire consequences usually accompany rash deeds."

"Words to live by."

"At least you know what's coming." He followed her into the living room. The sun was pouring over the balcony, the reflected light setting the tulip painting on the wall ablaze.

She turned to face him with a coolness bordering on hostility. He *was* a member of the Erskine family. "So what are you doing here? Boredom, filling in time before take-off?"

"Take-off is tomorrow first thing. I had an early morning visit from my grandfather."

"Trying to rein you in?"

"He's given up on that. But he wanted to make it quite clear that he's not pleased with me. He's not pleased with *you*. But that we know."

"Fancy that!" she said sarcastically. "Well, you know what they say—No good deed goes unpunished."

"Oscar Wilde."

"Certainly attributed to him. And didn't he get it right! It's also one of the primary rules of physics. Every force begets an equal and opposite force."

"So why don't we listen?" He let his eyes roam over her with pleasure. She hadn't changed out of her city clothes. She was wearing a very smart ensemble—a short black and white jacket cropped at the waist over a white silk blouse with some sort of ruffle down the front. The black skirt was tight and short, showcasing legs most women would die for.

"I was an excellent student," she said, without any fanfare

at all. "I did my dad and his memory proud. In being kind to me, Mr MacFarlane, you were bucking the system. The Erskine system, of which you are one of the main players. Surely you expected Grandpop to come back at you?"

"Oh, I was absolutely convinced he would," he said, showing no sign of worry. "Are you going to ask me to sit?"

She waved an expansive hand. "Take your pick."

"Any chance of a cup of coffee? That would be nice. Maybe a sandwich. Better yet, let me take you out for lunch."

"I think you've done enough damage, don't you?" Hang tough or not, she was shaking inside.

"Nonsense and let's cut back to first names. After all, we have been up close and personal. I was kind. Now I've done you damage?"

"I'm sorry. I did it all to myself. I threw caution to the winds. Not the best way to succeed in life. Come into the kitchen," she invited in a resigned tone. "We can discuss your plan there. Tell me how is Grandpop going to get square with *you*?"

"Disinherit me?" he suggested.

"That's wonderful," she crowed, then swiftly showed concern. "I'm only joking! What kind of a monster is he?"

"Put it this way. Hell will get hotter when he arrives."

"*That* bad?" She couldn't help but laugh.

"Some of the things he's done would have taken the Devil aback." He flashed her a smile that held more than a hint of the said devilment. Made a girl think white teeth and a great smile made the man. "Even if he disinherits you, you're rich too, aren't you?"

"Depends on what you call rich. I don't have Grandad's astro bucks but let's hear it for the MacFarlanes. The MacFarlanes don't need the Erskines. We do okay on our own."

"Well, that's great. So you're a race apart?"

"In a way." He glanced appreciatively around the shining kitchen—white with a yellow trim, polished golden timber floor, a couple of bright scatter rugs, big, sunny-face yellow gerberas arranged in a copper kettle. "Grandfather Erskine sees himself as the patriarch of the family. My own dad and my paternal grandfather are gone. I don't kowtow to my grandfather. I actually like him some of the time. I won't say he's a *lovely* man—"

"God forbid!" Amber shuddered, taking a container out of the refrigerator that held freshly ground coffee.

"But he's definitely got his good points."

"Naturally, that's not my view of him," she said in disgust.

"Give it time. He'll cool down."

"Are you saying I don't have to *stay* gone?"

"Not for ever," he said.

"Great! Only here's the tricky bit. In the meantime, he's made it impossible for me to get work."

"That's why I'm here." He pinned her with his crystal gaze. "I want to help."

"Pardon?" She lifted supercilious brows. The cool ease was getting to her. It shouted money. Lots of it. A life of privilege, though she didn't doubt for a moment he worked hard. That showed as well.

"Hear me out." His voice was smooth and reassuring. A voice one listened to.

"How can you help when you've just told me your grandfather is furious at your apparent support of me thus far? He would see it as an additional act of gross disloyalty."

"Let's forget my grandfather. He doesn't figure in this."

"That's all right for you to say! But I have nowhere else to turn. For the time being, anyway. The word has gone out. Wyatt's finished in the business."

"Look, do you want *me* to make the coffee?" he asked as progress on that front had stopped.

"God, you're a piece of work!" she muttered. "You just sit there." She shrugged out of her jacket, placing it carefully over the back of a chair. Had she known in advance she was going to be sacked she would never have bought such an expensive outfit.

"I thought you wanted to be a writer?" he was saying, sliding onto one of the high bar stools along the counter. She suddenly saw him as what he was. The Cattle Baron. A man of the great outdoors. He was superbly fit, every movement full of languid grace and perfect co-ordination. The fact that he looked particularly good in formal clothes was just an added bonus. His body gave class to whatever he wore.

"I hadn't intended to start quite so soon." She spooned coffee into the stainless steel basket. "But hang on. Maybe I can get a grant from the Arts Council? Unless Gramps has influence there too?"

"How do you know your chance doesn't await you right now?" he countered.

She gave him a long considering look. "You're telling me to go for broke?"

"You must have a little money put aside?"

"Hey, I'm not in your league. I'm probably somewhere between broke and doing nicely provided I have a steady income. I lease this apartment. I don't *own* it."

He looked back, a slight frown between his strongly marked brows. "I bet your landlord loves you. I'd say you make the perfect tenant. Only they allow you to hang all the paintings on the wall? Holes in the plaster and so forth?"

She stared back with frosty eyes. "Sure the Body Corporate didn't send you?" She waved the spoon, like a teacher with a cane. "A good friend of mine bought the apartment for an investment—"

"And he's allowed you to rent it." He nodded as though he quite understood.

"Who said it was a *he*?" She came close to throwing the spoon.

"Just a lucky guess."

"You're not improving my temper, MacFarlane," she warned.

"Why so aggressive all of a sudden?" He threw up his hands. "Though I bet you're a real firecracker when you get going. I meant no offence, ma'am. Just a guess."

"I'm not a firecracker. I have a lovely nature." For some reason a tear slid down her cheek.

"Why, Amber!" He stood up immediately, radiating warmth and a comforting male presence.

"Don't you dare touch me!" She dashed at her eyes. "That tear got away from me. It's anger, by the way."

"Sure. Let me finish that off." He walked around the counter, took the percolator off her, screwed it together tightly, then set it on the hotplate.

She stood for a moment watching him. Everything he did was so precise. "You must really need that cup of coffee."

"I didn't get one for breakfast so I'm suffering withdrawal."

"So what's the plan?" She was desperate to hear it. She busied herself setting out coffee cups and saucers. Fortunately, she had some very fancy chocolate biscuits on hand, though she went easy on biscuits and cakes.

"One I'm sure is going to lift your spirits. At least I hope it does." He turned to face her, his green eyes alight. "How would you like a long vacation on one of the nation's premier cattle stations? You said you wanted to write. Start your saga there. Colleen McCullough used a sheep station for one of her settings in *The Thorn Birds*. Why not a cattle station? Jingala has a lot to offer. Have you ever been Outback?"

She didn't think she could sustain the epic pace.

"Well, *have* you?"

"I'm too amazed—nay too *grateful*—to speak."

"So you accept my offer?"

She took a deep breath, her voice unsteady. "I didn't say that at all. I said—"

"You were grateful. Think about it. You'll come as my guest. That means you won't have to find a cent. You didn't answer my question. Have you visited the Red Centre, the Channel Country, the Kimberley?"

She gazed back at him, turning a little pink. "I think I've seen more of Europe than my own country, outside the big cities and tropical North Queensland. Now I'm ashamed to say it."

"As you should be." The censure was unmistakable. "So now's the time to discover the real Australia. I promise you it will be an experience you won't forget."

"I'm sure." She was feeling more agitated than she thought possible. A friend had recently come back from the Alice and had found the trip to the Centre and its great monuments fabulous. "Listen, I'm still stunned." She looked right at him. "I take it there'll be no hanky panky?"

"Absolutely not! Unless *you* want it. Seriously, I was brought up a gentleman, Ms Wyatt. *No* from a woman and I'm gone! Out of there!"

"I bet there've been precious few nos," she said sharply.

"A gentleman doesn't tell. If you can be ready, we can leave in the morning."

She held up a hand. "Whoa, there! I'm still too dumb-founded to give you an answer."

The coffee had begun to perk. "That's okay. I don't want to rush you. Take your time. But I'll need to know before I leave."

The pure utter simplicity of the idea!

CHAPTER FIVE

AMBER'S trips up and down the Eastern Seaboard, to the North Queensland rainforest and the Great Barrier Reef, marvellous wine country in New South Wales, Victoria and South Australia, the great cities of the world—nothing had even given her a glimpse into what was the Great Australian Outback. The sheer dimensions were overwhelming. The isolation frightening. It was like looking out at the world at the time of Creation, with no human habitation. Wilderness fanned out to eternity…

She had been concentrating so much on the journey her head felt tight. The Cattle Baron sat beside her at the controls, splendidly serene. Flying his own plane was a piece of cake to him. Equivalent to her taking a cab. She was very grateful to him. He had offered her salvation. For a time, anyway. An unexpected chance to do what she had always wanted to do since she had been caught up as a child into the wonderful realm of books:

Write one herself.

She'd had ideas mulling around in her head for years. She didn't expect to measure up to her great favourites, but she thought she could turn out something that might rate getting published. In her heart she welcomed and embraced this extraordinary chance. And what a setting! She already had the sense of great *separation*. This was another world from the lush Eastern seaboard. She would be seeing the Interior through fresh, marvelling eyes. She would be seeing it too through *his* eyes. This was Cal MacFarlane's world. He had offered her escape and a chance. Now it was up to her. The shock and unexpectedness of it all had shoved the extremes of being jilted, the public humiliation and the loss of her job right to the back of her mind. Truth be known, she felt down-right energised!

They were on the last lap of the journey, flying into the MacFarlanes' desert fortress, Jingala. It must have been a phenomenal slog to have achieved so much in this place that few people to this day had ever seen. Over the long journey she had witnessed the landscape totally changing its charac-ter. Now its most striking feature, apart from the empty im-mensity, was the dry, vibrating colour. And what colour! It was spectacular. The great vault of the sky was a vigorous cobalt-blue. It contrasted wonderfully with the flaming orange-red of an ancient land that pulsed in oven-baked heat. The rolling red sand dunes surrounding it were a source of fascination. They ran in endless parallel waves with the anti-clockwise rhythm of the wind curling them over at the top, mimicking the waves of the legendary sea of pre-history.

Spinifex, burnt gold and shaped like spherical bales, gave the impression of the greatest crop ever sown on earth. The mirage she had heard so much about lay beneath them like silvery quivering bolts of material that seemed to change form and shape as she watched. Trees grew in the arid terrain, gnarled and twisted into living sculptures. She could easily spot the ghost gums with their blazing white boles. This was Dreamtime country. Venerable.

As they descended, she caught the full dazzle of chain after chain of billabongs, some silver, some palest blue like aquamarine, others the cool green of the Cattle Baron's eyes. These lakes, waterholes, billabongs and breakaway gullies were the lifeblood of this riverine desert called the Channel Country that lay deep into the South-West pocket of the giant State of Queensland, bordering the great Simpson Desert. She knew it was second only to the Sahara in area.

Thick belts of trees marked the course of the maze of waterways that snaked across the landscape. From the air, the foliage appeared to be more a light-reflecting gun-metal grey than green. She could see kangaroos in their hundreds bounding their way across the desert sands. Her eyes could pick up camels too. She knew they were not indigenous to Australia. Outback camels, progeny of the camels brought into the country by their Afghan handlers as beasts of burden for the Outback's trackless regions, had thrived and multiplied to some seven hundred thousand. Some said this was a bad thing. Camels were long-lived and they did so much damage to the fragile desert environment. Others went along with a live and let live policy. There was something rather romantic about them, she thought, but she could well see the serious side of the problem.

Acutely alert to everything coming up before her, she had her first sight of Jingala's great herds. She couldn't begin to count the number of head in one area alone. A smallish section of the herd was being watered at a creek. She could see camps alongside. Whole collections of holding camps, cattle packed in, men on the ground, men on horseback, supply vehicles. Not so far off, wild horses were galloping at breakneck speed, a stallion most likely in the lead, the others running four abreast. What a thrilling sight! City born and bred, it was just as well she was at home on a horse. She might not have rated an invitation had she said she was scared of horses, as a lot of people were. Horses were very unpredictable animals. She had taken a few spills in her time, mercifully without major injury.

MacFarlane gestured to her.

The homestead was coming up.

Her first thought as they were coming in to land was that they were arriving at a desert outpost that a small colony of intrepid settlers had made their home. The silver roof of a giant hangar was glittering fiercely in the sun, emblazoned with the legend Jingala. Beyond that, outbuildings painted white to throw off the sun fanned out in a broad circle surrounding a green oasis that had to be the home compound. She could see a huge dark bluish tiled roof, roughly three times the size of any city mansion. But so far no real sighting of the actual house. A line of dark amethyst hills in the distance took her eye. They had eroded into fantastic shapes with the shimmering veil of mirage thrown over them. The brightness of it all was splintering her eyes. The far-off hill country, though of no great height, by comparison with the endless flat plains served as the most spectacular backdrop. It was paradise in its own strange way. Even at this early stage, it was already establishing a grip on her. Hard to believe the continent had once been covered in rainforest. That was one hundred million years ago. But still a blip in geological time.

Never for a moment of the trip had she felt an instant's fear, though she had heard plenty of scary tales about light aircraft crashes in the wilds of the rugged Outback. Something about desert thermals bouncing light aircraft around. She would have to ask the Cattle Baron. As expected, he was a fine pilot. She guessed he was a fine just about everything. And a devilishly handsome man. After her sad experience, she was determined she wasn't going to be swept away by his undoubted charisma. Better to turn the cheek than do the kissing. A whole lot safer too.

After hours in the air, they were ready to land…

The homestead itself was an unforgettable sight. She had expected the sort of colonial architecture she had seen in the big coffee table books, the rather grandiose mansions of the Western Districts of Victoria or South Australia, reminders of Home that almost exclusively had been the British Isles, maybe the classical architecture of New South Wales and Tasmania, but what confronted her was *her* idea of a great country house that wouldn't have been out of place in South East Asia. She had enjoyed several trips to Thailand. The house put her in mind of that part of the world and she said as much to the Cattle Baron.

He gave her a smile that brought her out in the trembles. "You got it in one. A big section of the original homestead was destroyed by fire in the late nineteen-forties. My grandfather razed what remained to the ground, then brought in a friend of his, a Thai prince he had met on his travels, who was also an architect, to design the new homestead. It's a one-off for our neck of the woods."

"And it's wonderful," she said. "Not at all what I expected. You should have peacocks patrolling the grounds."

"Maybe we can rise to a few emus."

"You can't tame emus, surely?"

"Yes, you can," he said, watching her. He had set her a number of little tests to gauge her reactions when removed from her comfort zone. She had passed all of them with flying colours. He didn't know if he was pleased or the fact bothered him. This astonishingly beautiful woman belonged in the city, surely? That was her future. Jingala was a far cry from anything she was used to. His mother couldn't hack it.

She was staring up into his face, noting the darkening change of expression. "I never know if you're serious or fooling."

"You'll know when I'm serious."

Some note in his voice had her flushing. To hide it, she turned away, resuming her study of this fascinating and totally unexpected house. For all its size, it sat unobtrusively in its oasis of a setting, which she put down to the fact that it was constructed almost entirely of dark-stained timber.

"The pyramid form is exactly right."

"Glad you like it. Five in all, as you can see, with broad overhangs to shelter the upper verandas. The central section is the largest. It acts as a portico."

"So you have a group of separate places."

He nodded. "What we call the Great Room is the common room, our reception room."

"I recognise the Khmer style. I've been to Thailand three or four times. The roof and window treatment, the timber grilles and framework are all recognisably Khmer style."

"Educated eyes, obviously."

She glanced up at him to see if there was mockery involved. Even then she wasn't sure. "The house is perfect for the tropics, yet it appears equally well at home in the desert. Not that everything around us resembles a desert. The grounds are thriving."

"We had a wonderful drenching over the cooler months. But we do have an underground source of water from the Great Artesian Basin. My great-grandmother saw to it that the grounds were heavily planted out with date palms and desert oaks. She was one smart lady, all the way from the Scottish Highlands. The other trees and plants were selected to cope with the hot dry environment."

"You must tell me about this clever great-grandmother of yours," she said. "That's when you have the time."

"Ms Wyatt, I'll make time," he said with considerable aplomb. "We'll go inside. Surely you're feeling the heat of the sun?" Amazingly, she looked as if she wasn't feeling it one bit. In fact, she looked magnolia-cool.

"It *is* hot," she agreed. "But I can tolerate *dry* heat. It's the humidity of the tropics that gets to me. Anyway, being a redhead, I always use sunblock."

"And a good wide brimmed hat would be very helpful. You've packed one, I hope?" He frowned slightly.

"Well, I didn't have time to race out to buy an Akubra, if that's what you mean. But I threw in a couple of decent broad brimmed hats."

"Thank God for that! I can only hope and pray our Outback does nothing to harm that exquisite skin. Tell me, did you *ever* have freckles?"

The way he looked at her caused little sparkles in her blood. Not that there was anything overtly sexual about it. He just happened to be a very sexy man, which wasn't all that easy for even a good-looking man to pull off. "It may be news, but the answer is no," she said lightly. "I don't know that my mother ever let me out of the house without a hat. I was never able to bask beachside, for instance. But I don't crinkle and wrinkle in the sun either. Why, are you disappointed I don't have a few freckles?"

He laughed. "The short answer is no. So come into the house. Chips, one of our groundsmen, will attend to your luggage and bring it to your room."

"I *am* expected?" She tilted her head to look up at him. It was a great feeling.

"Of course you're expected," he said.

"How good is that!"

The housekeeper, Dee, early fifties, dressed uniform style in crisp navy and white checked cotton, showed her to her room. Dee was a small, wry, smiling woman with a pretty cap of salt and pepper curls, velvety dark eyes and a copper skin. Amber guessed she was highly efficient. She gave the impression of being a durable sort of woman. A woman one could depend on. From her colouring and a certain lilt in her speech, Amber thought she might also have aboriginal blood in her. Later, she was to find out that it was through Dee's maternal grandmother.

"I hope you like where I've put you, miss," Dee was saying, turning to gesture to the tall lanky man with a head like a bald tyre who suddenly appeared with Amber's luggage in hand. This had to be Chips. "Just beside the bed, thanks, Chips." Chips nodded, giving Amber lots of curious looks, almost as a child would.

"Leave 'em, dear," Dee continued in a brisk motherly tone. "God bless."

Chips deposited the luggage where told, then reached out to shake Dee's hand. "Bless you, Dee. You're a lovely person."

Dee took his arm and began to walk him to the door. "You're a lovely person too."

"That was Chips," Dee said when she returned from seeing him off. "If you wondered why I didn't introduce you, Chips would have plonked himself down on the bed and told you the story of his life. Not a happy one until he arrived on Jingala. He's a good bloke is Chips. He used to be a stockman, but he took a terrible kick to the head from his horse. Its name was Lazy May, believe it or not, six and more years ago. Since then he's been a little slow, but talkative if you know what I mean. Once he gets started, it's hard to get him to stop."

"But he's got a good home."

"We *all* have." Dee gave a heartfelt exhalation. "The MacFarlanes have always been revered the length and breadth of the Outback. Cal is the best there is. Now, want me to unpack for you?'

Amber smiled. "Thanks, Dee, but I can manage. I'm sure you've got other things to do. And please do call me Amber."

"Beautiful name for a beautiful woman," Dee announced, giving Amber's face and bright mane of hair a worried glance. "You're gonna have to watch yourself out here, Amber. I'd hate to see you burn. You the redhead an' all with that lovely skin."

"I'll take care," Amber said. "My colouring isn't as fragile as it looks."

Dee laid a hand briefly on Amber's arm. "I'll look around for an Akubra," she said. "Got a whole bunch o' hats for guests and the like. Lunch in a half hour. Mrs MacFarlane not so good today. So you mightn't see her. Had a real bad night with the little fella. I've given up offering to watch him. We don't get on so good and I get on with most people. That's me and the young Mrs MacFarlane, that is. I have to say she's got herself one difficult little soul. Doesn't want to be held. Doesn't even want to eat. Cries all the time, poor little scrap. Mrs MacFarlane is kinda delicate, high-strung, and it's communicating itself to the little fella, in my opinion. Not that I ever had any kids, I'm sorry to say. Me fiancé, Des, was killed in the big stampede nearly thirty years ago. So that was that! Just thought I'd fill you in. Ya have to know."

"And I appreciate it, Dee." From what she had seen of the easy-going Dee, Amber had to wonder just how nerve-ridden Jan MacFarlane was. "Cal did mention about the baby," she said, finding his first name strange on her tongue. This guy was an Outback prince! "Mrs MacFarlane is suffering post-natal depression?" she asked. "Life must be very harrowing for someone going through such a trauma. So many cases reported lately."

Dee nodded. "Celebrities coming forward to tell of their experiences."

"In the hope it might help other young mothers in the same situation. It must ease the burden and anxiety to know you're not alone. Others suffer and come through." She had sensed a certain lack of empathy in the Cattle Baron. She didn't expect it in this nice motherly woman. It could be difficult for a man—especially a man of action blessed with superb health—to properly understand how badly a woman could suffer from PND. But why wasn't Dee more openly sympathetic? "There isn't a nanny to help out?" Obviously there was money to burn.

"Two ex-nurses-cum-nannies came and went. Experienced, capable women, especially the second, Martha. Unfortunately, Mrs MacFarlane made them feel bad," she confided with a hint of grimness. "She's just come unstuck. Not every woman is a mothering kinda woman. She won't have any of my girls, my house girls, good girls, look after the little fella. Not good enough. It used to be called racial discrimination."

"Surely not?" Amber was appalled.

"Beyond reason!" Dee shrugged. "She wouldn't let me even pick 'im up for a good while until things got too tough and Cal had to step in."

"But what about her husband?" Amber asked, feeling dismay for mother and child.

Dee gave a sad smile. "Mr Eliot is a lovely man. He adored Miss Caroline, but she died of breast cancer. We didn't think anyone would ever come along to measure up. But then he met Mrs MacFarlane at a big fund-raiser in Melbourne. She had some job in finance. Worked for a merchant bank. It was a kinda whirlwind affair. Cal didn't even meet her until the wedding. Small and quiet. I think she thought Mr Eliot would buy a place in Melbourne so they could settle there. They couldn't have discussed it because Mr Eliot's heart is here. He's terribly distressed about it all but he's kinda useless in this type of situation. And Mrs MacFarlane!" Dee lifted her narrow shoulders. "You'll see."

With Dee gone, Amber looked around her, her mind awhirl. So even in Paradise there was trouble. Her accommodation, however, was everything she could have wished and dreamed. She had been given a beautiful room—it was big, bright and airy, with the characteristic Asian elegance and simplicity. The colour scheme was subtle—brown, beige and white with colour coming from silk cushions and the beautiful rugs on the dark polished floor. She sat on the canopy bed, staring upwards.

It was very romantic. She tried a few bounces. Lovely! The bed was made of ebony, draped in mosquito netting with a heavy ivory satin flounce to match the flounce on the canopy. The timber floor simply glowed. There was a long antique Asian chest at the foot of the bed, two teak tub chairs and a big comfortable day bed upholstered in white cotton with brown and white scatter cushions. As a touch of whimsy, near the shuttered doors was a wooden camel, honey-gold in colour, about four feet high with topaz glass eyes. She loved it.

She stayed where she was for a few more minutes, soaking everything in, then she rose from the bed to inspect the workmanlike desk and chair in another corner, exquisite ivory lilliums in a glass vase standing on the desk's surface. She wondered if the desk had been installed especially for her. Directly outside the series of open shutter doors were some densely planted green shrubs of much the same height, she later found out to her astonishment were Camellia sinensis. In other words, tea. She had thought the crop required a tropical environment with high rainfall. The bushes she was looking at appeared to be thriving in a place that rarely saw rain. She wondered if all those soft green shoots were ever plucked. It was all so exotic, so wildly incongruous, she couldn't wait to begin her desert adventure. Her image of the charming, debonair Sean, who had so badly let her down, was fading daily under this battery of change and excitement.

The thought struck her that *she* was good with children. Maybe in some way she could help out? A problem existed. Another thought popped up. Could that have anything to do with the Cattle Baron inviting her to stay? Was she to fill the post of nurse-nanny? Was it too churlish to wonder? Two nannies had come and gone. Was she Nanny Number three?

Don't be ridiculous, girl. She chided herself for the thought. The invitation had nothing whatsoever to do with the current crisis.

Could it? she see-sawed. Why he hadn't even asked her if she was good with kids? A fit person in every sense of the word. She was being plain silly. And cynical. It wasn't the Cattle Baron's crisis anyway. Little Marcus's mother and father had to address their own problems. Help was available. Favourable results were on record.

She headed to the stylish en-suite bathroom, which was stocked with everything she could possibly want for the fore-seeable future, to take a quick shower to freshen up after the long trip. The Cattle Baron had promised to show her around as much as he could of the vast station.

Vive Le Cattle Baron!

She was hardly out of her room in the east wing on her way downstairs to the living area when she heard raised voices much further down the wide corridor. The polished floor was partially covered with a jewel-toned Persian runner which muted her footsteps. Correction: she heard *one* raised voice— a woman's, head-splittingly emotional, and the low rumble of a man's. What to do? Pop back into her room? For the life of her she couldn't move…

"Jan, *please*…" The male voice, closer this time, was full of anguish and pleading.

Better to go forward than backwards. Amber pinched herself and moved on.

"I swear to God I'm going crazy! I don't know what to do. I never thought it would be like this. I wish I'd never married you. I wish you'd never talked me into having a baby. I only did it to please you. I hated being pregnant, big and bulging, my figure ruined, my breasts turned to marshmallow. I don't *want* babies. I don't want this one. It's not normal. All it can do is cry."

A door must have opened because now Amber could hear a baby screaming. She winced. It had to be filling its little lungs with painful pockets of air. The sound was heartbreaking and, she had to admit, very hard on the nerves.

The low rumble again in response. The next moment a tall, spare man with a gentlemanly elegant air stepped into the corridor. Frozen in place, Amber met his deeply troubled eyes. They were bright blue in his tanned face. Though the colour of the eyes was different, she could see the strong family resemblance between Eliot MacFarlane and his nephew.

It was a bad moment. "I'm so sorry," Amber found herself apologizing. "I'm Amber Wyatt, Mr MacFarlane. Cal invited me to stay. I was just on my way down to lunch." She hastened to move on, not wanting to embarrass him further, but his wife, looking more like his daughter, and holding a screaming baby, made a rush through the open doorway at him, leaving Amber fearing she was going to throw him the distressed little bundle.

"That's right! Go and leave me," she shouted with a kind of withering contempt. "Go on. That's all you're good for, Eliot. Shut me out."

Eliot MacFarlane didn't answer. He looked unbearably embarrassed. It was then that his wife spotted the agonised Amber. "Who the devil are you?" she demanded in a tone of voice one wouldn't use with a masked intruder.

"For goodness' sake, Jan, this is Ms Wyatt, Cal's house guest," Eliot MacFarlane broke in, sounding seriously horrified.

"Right!" Jan MacFarlane's acknowledging laugh had nothing to do with good humour. "You haven't struck us at a good moment, Ms Wyatt, as you can see. You married?"

"No." Amber shook her head. She had arranged her hair in little side plaits, with a thick plait to hang down her back.

"It's not what it's cracked up to be." Jan MacFarlane spoke bitterly, still studying Amber in detail. "I'm not myself any more."

Amber was trying hard to imagine what "myself" was like.

Janis MacFarlane was good-looking, as the Cattle Baron had told her, but devoid of any hint of softness or warmth. She had long dark hair, huge dark brown eyes that dominated a fine-boned face. Thin enough to be anorexic.

"Would you like me to take the baby for a moment, Mrs MacFarlane?" Amber offered. The poor little scrap was scarlet in the face, little arms clawing the air. He was clearly deeply distressed. That really smote Amber's tender heart.

"Sure. Take him. But to where?" That bitter laugh again. "I'd say he comes from hell."

"That's unforgivable, Jan," Eliot MacFarlane protested, looking utterly mortified. He let his hand rest lightly on his little son's head.

Amber reached them in a flash. Janis MacFarlane was a teenie bit scary, maybe self-obsessed. "Here, give him to me, Mrs MacFarlane. Dee told me you'd had a bad night. You should rest." Gripped by compassion, she took the little bundle that was all but thrust at her. Marcus MacFarlane's tiny face was all bunched up, flushed scarlet with the effects of exertion.

"Hey, little fellow. You're in some distress, aren't you? Hey, little Marcus?" she began to croon, hoping the gentleness in her voice would take effect. She had soothed friends' babies plenty of times but this little fellow's cries had a different ring. She began to walk, putting the baby very gently over her shoulder, holding him firmly and rubbing his tiny back. "You must stop crying now, little man. Everything is going to be just fine. Stop crying now, Marcus." She rubbed and patted as she spoke. "You'll see."

Busy calming the baby with her back to the others, she didn't see Cal MacFarlane stride up the staircase, his body language tense. He was quickly followed up by Dee, kneading an apron.

"Well, I never!" Dee exclaimed, eyeing the spectacle of nurturing woman and child. "The little guy likes you, Amber," she said with relief, studying the pinched little face inclined over Amber's shoulder. They had heard the baby's crying. It had gone on more or less non-stop for months. Now, incredibly, the crying had turned off like a tap and the baby was making a grab for Amber's red-gold and copper plait.

"For two minutes, I'd say!" Incredibly, Jan MacFarlane sounded so furious with Amber's success she might have been jealous.

The Cattle Baron sloughed a heavy sigh. "Lovely! We came to collect you for lunch, Amber."

"And I'll be there. I'm hungry." Amber resettled the baby in her arms, enormously glad the little fellow had settled, if only for the time being. The angry red was leaving his small face, leaving isolated blotches that looked so pathetic that tears sprang into her eyes. Marcus at this stage didn't appear to have inherited his parents' good looks, but he was staring up at Amber as if to say, *This is the way I want to be held.*

"Maybe Marcus can come with us?" she suggested, meeting the Cattle Baron's ultra-cool eyes. She was wary of putting Marcus down, even warier of handing him back to his mother. "He seems to have settled now. He can lie beside us while we eat?" She waited for approval, in the next breath realizing she should have looked to the baby's parents.

"Well, we can give it a try." Cal was as surprised and grateful as Dee. "You're joining us?" He looked to his uncle.

"You go, Eliot." Janis MacFarlane all but spat the words, as though she would be better off without him. "Ms Wyatt is right. I need to rest."

"See you soon," Cal MacFarlane said smoothly, but with a saturnine edge to his voice.

A fearful worry from birth, little Marcus, to all appearances, was thoroughly intrigued by the new woman in his life, especially her warming, glowing red hair. He lay on the floor

beside Amber in his bouncinette, which she kept rocking from
time to time with a little movement of her foot.

This is nothing short of a miracle, Cal was thinking. It
was clear the beautiful Ms Wyatt loved babies and babies
loved her. Maybe the gentleness of her manner, the soft
crooning voice—she had a lovely voice, which would have
worked well for her on television—and the beauty of her
person was central to the big turnaround. He could see his
uncle was so grateful he had tears in his eyes. Like little
Marc, Eliot had taken a shine to their guest. The real tragedy
was that Jan wasn't trying an inch. She was tremendously
self-involved. In his judgement, it was part of her character. So when did the baby blues end and this post-natal depression begin? As a condition, it was a curse. But did
every sufferer set out to be nasty to everyone they came in
contact with? Was Jan by nature nasty? Cal didn't think nas-
tiness was specific to the condition they kept going on
about. He was no expert on such matters, but he knew Jan
had held down a very good job in the world of finance
before her marriage—she was highly intelligent—but
directly after the civil ceremony she had begun acting as if
she had married into royalty. How Eliot had never spotted
her social ambitions during their all too brief courtship he
didn't know. Not that he was any expert either at spotting
the flaws in women. Brooke was trying pretty hard to make
a comeback. No chance!

*"Just a moment of madness, darling. I was so lonely
without you and Chris was there. Love had nothing to do
with it. It was just sex, which was pretty damned ordinary.
Nothing like you and me."*

Talk about an excuse! At least Brooke had her own money,
the only daughter of a fellow station owner. Jan had expected
that she and Eliot would settle down in Melbourne, where
she could swan around enjoying Eliot's not inconsiderable

fortune. The honeymoon had lasted six months of luxurious
world travel, but he knew how much his uncle had missed
Jingala. He was a MacFarlane. It was in his blood.

Lunch consisted of a delicious tomato and goat's cheese tart
with wonderful flaky puff pastry, and a beautifully crisp green
salad with just the right dressing. It went down well. Baby
Marcus remained calm and at peace as though all he ever
needed was to be with people, having his bouncinette gently
rocked. With coffee Dee, aided by her well-trained, part-abo-
riginal helper, Mina, a gentle, pretty young girl aged around
sixteen, served another delectable tart, nectarine this time,
oozing fruit, with a scoop of ice cream. Normally Amber didn't
do sweets for lunch but this time she made an exception.

"So what now?" Cal asked, readying himself for just about
anything. Ms Wyatt might very well elect to bring the baby
on their tour of the station. Talk about a woman who used her
own initiative!

Unaware of his wry admiration Amber looked down at the
baby in the bouncinette, a considering expression on her face.
"I think our little Marcus might sleep. Look, his breathing is
giving way to a nice easy rhythm. Isn't that lovely? I wouldn't
even take him out of the bouncinette. What do you think, Dee?"

"I'm with you, love," Dee answered with a nod of approval,
as though she had known Amber all her life. Eliot looked happy
but slightly bemused. Why couldn't Janis get this result?

She had only been on Jingala a matter of hours, yet Ms
Wyatt appeared very much at home, Cal thought. She had Dee
and his uncle on side. In fact a visitor would assume she was
very much part of the family. It had its piquant side.

"I can sit and watch him," Eliot MacFarlane volunteered,
even though Cal could see his uncle was uneasy about the
outcome. Baby Marcus had screamed non-stop almost from
birth.

"See, his eyes are closing," Amber pointed out with a lovely tender smile.

Eliot's breath whistled. If only. If only. "Poor wee mite hasn't been getting any sleep at all. My wife is a total wreck. It's been *very* hard on her."

"So what is she going to do about it?" Cal tried hard not to show his impatience. He knew all about "baby blues". He was godfather to quite a few kids. But this was something else again. Something he couldn't put his finger on.

So what then was it? The marriage wasn't working out. He already knew that. The age difference? It wasn't all that great. What exactly was causing Jan's nonstop lashing out at anyone within earshot? He suspected she had always been a bit on the emotionally unstable side. Even before she'd fallen pregnant his uncle had told him Jan was given to mood swings. He really wanted to be sympathetic. He didn't enjoy seeing anyone suffering but his own assessment, backed by a top nurse from the Royal Flying Doctor Service, was that Jan was furiously disappointed her life wasn't working out as she had planned.

"Mainly Mrs MacFarlane doesn't want to take on the role of mother. Not everyone is cut out to be a parent, you know."

Like he needed to be told! He had the miserable experience of his own runaway mother.

Amber, her eyes trained on the Cattle Baron's high mettled face, could see the banked-down rage, impatience, frustration, whatever, behind his controlled exterior. Fabulous though he was, he appeared to be lacking in sympathy, which didn't win him a batch of Brownie points from her. Then she felt ashamed. He had been very sympathetic in relation to her; that didn't appear to be the case with his aunt by marriage. A bit weird to think that Jan MacFarlane was only a few years older than he was.

"Why don't we find you a comfortable chair, Eliot?" She swiftly intervened. He had asked her almost immediately to call him by his Christian name. Warmth and friendliness rarely failed.

"Yeah, let's fix you up," said Dee.

They had been dining in a lovely relaxed place, an informal area off the kitchen. Tall, timber framed glass doors were folded concertina fashion to give the spacious seating area the effect of a breezy veranda where the indoors met up with the outdoors. The view across the grounds, liberally dotted with majestic date palms and desert oaks, stretched away to the mirage-shrouded hills that had lightened by the hour to a dusky pink. She had read about this changing of colour of the great rocks of the Interior, especially Uluru and Kata Tjunta that was said to be spectacular. Now she was in this part of the world, she wondered why she had never made the trek to the Centre. Her career and other destinations had kept getting in the way.

They rose from the table as one but it was Cal who gently took hold of little Marcus in his bouncinette and gestured to Amber rather imperiously, she thought, to select her idea of the suitable chair for his uncle to mind baby. It was all she could do not to bob a curtsy.

"I'll have a bottle of formula ready," Dee whispered, placing an encouraging hand on Amber's shoulder.

Marcus made no protest as his bouncinette was lowered to the floor beside the comfortable armchair Amber chose. It was close to an antique Asian chest with quite an accumulation of interesting-looking books piled on top of it. Eliot would have something to read, though he too looked as if he was in desperate need of sleep.

The manoeuvre successful, Cal resisted the temptation to give Ms Wyatt a sardonic salute. At the very least, her coming had brought a breath of sanity. That took some doing. But what next? He hadn't invited her to Jingala to fill the role of nanny. He just hoped she knew that.

CHAPTER SIX

NO SOONER had Amber taken her seat in the four-wheel drive than he took off like a rocket.

"Hey, what is this, lift-off?" she yelped. She had been comfortably settling herself in, enveloped in a warm glow of excitement and anticipation, now she had to scramble to secure her seat belt.

"We've got a lot of ground to cover." He turned his dark head to give her a challenging smile. "Hold still now. We're going to do a lot of winding in, out and over some pretty rough terrain, fording a creek or two. Why, are you terrified already?"

"Gosh, I thought I looked relaxed."

"You don't."

"Darn and I was trying to make a good impression. Might be a stupid question, but are there any crocs in your lagoons?"

"Ms Wyatt, I don't want to have to rope in your level of IQ."

"Nothing wrong with my IQ. A friend of mine was chased by a croc up at Mount Isa where crocs shouldn't be."

He laughed. "Somebody introduced saltwater crocs into a dam up there when they were babies. They survived in fresh water. There would have been a sign about that your friend obviously ignored."

"He said not. He had multiple lacerations trying to get through the barbed wire."

"Barbed wire, really?" He glanced at her with sparkling eyes. "Barbed wire generally means, *Stay Out*, Ms Wyatt."

"Great! I've got that right," she answered dryly.

"One learns best when under threat."

"Words to live by," she drawled, then broke off in amazement. "Oh, look at the birds!" She stared out of the window at a fantastic V-shaped formation of tiny emerald-and-gold winged bodies. "Budgies," she proclaimed, absolutely delighted with the massed display. "There must be *thousands* of them."

"A common sight around here," he told her, secretly very pleased by her enthusiasm and the radiance of her expression. "You're in the land of parrots, the sulphur-crested cockatoos, the pink and grey galahs, the millions of chats and wrens and finches. The pretty little zebra finches—you'll spot them from the stripes—form the staple diet of the hawks and falcons, sad to say, but that's the wilds. The predators just swoop down very leisurely to collect their prey."

"So, these zebra chats? Black stripes on a white body or white stripes on a black body?"

"Are you serious?" He headed cross country for the glinting chain of lagoons.

"I kid you not."

"Damned if I know," he said. "I've lived here all my life and I've never given it a thought."

"That's okay. I guess you're too busy. I'll check it out."

"Check out our biggest bird while you're at it."

"Wedge-tailed eagle, right?"

He nodded. "Listen, you should have come out here sooner. I can see you're going to make a great student of Outback flora and fauna. You'll see plenty of eagles, especially up in the ridges. I'm thrilled you're so interested in our bird life. A couple of months back when the channels were in flood the nomadic water birds arrived from all over. Countless thousands of them. Jingala is a major breeding ground, as are the other big Channel Country stations. There are huge colonies of ibis. Hundreds of birds in one colony. They nest in the lignum swamps. The pelicans love isolation so they pick the most remote lagoons to make their nests. Then you have spoonbills, shags, herons, water hens, ducks of all kinds. You can see them gathered in great numbers at any waterhole. Water birds are nomads. They have to be. When the water dries up they fly off to better country."

"And I've missed them," she said regretfully, struck anew by the beauty of the mirage. It was pulsing away like a silvery fire amid the green line of trees.

"They haven't *all* gone," he assured her. "So buck up. Jingala will fulfil its promise, Ms Wyatt. You won't be starved for the sight of birds. There's still plenty of water around. We've had more glorious rain than we've had in a very long time. The most prolific display of wildflowers is over. You would have loved it, but there are still areas covered in paper daisies and a lot of beautiful little spider lilies near the banks of the billabongs. The water lilies flower all the time. They're quite magnificent. Oddly enough, some of the most exquisite little flowers bloom in the arid soil and the rocky pockets of the hill country. I'll show you another day. The hardiest plant, virtually indestructible, is the spinifex, which you see growing all around us. The reason the spinifex survives is because the root system is always shaded from the sun. See all the long vertical spikes?"

Amber looked out with interest at the great golden clumps that formed a thick three hundred and sixty degree circle. "Yes."

"They have a waxy coating to prevent moisture loss. Even a scorching sun is thrown off by the pointed tips, while the roots are protected.'

"So the spinifex is perfectly adapted to this incredible environment. What I'm finding so unusual are the endless chains of billabongs. It's the desert but not the desert. It's like magic."

"It's a riverine desert," he corrected. "When the big floods are on and the water is brought down from the monsoonal tropical North through our inland river system, the Diamantina, the Georgina and Cooper's Creek, those same billabongs we're heading for can run fifty miles across."

"Good grief!" She tried to visualize such a scene. "Now that's downright scary. Have you ever been marooned?"

He turned his head to look squarely into the golden lakes of her eyes. "Of course. It's drought or flood, Amber. We have to live with both. Many have died in the struggle. Every one of us, right from the first days of settlement, have had to make huge sacrifices. I love my country—this country around us—with a passion. I love it—I wouldn't want to be anywhere else—but the one thing you couldn't call it is *safe*. There are always huge hazards, danger all around you. So don't go getting too carried away."

"Is that a warning?" she asked, her eyes on a solitary conical shaped rock formation standing like a beacon amid the spinifex.

His eyes glittered. "I'm just putting you straight. How would a woman with apricot hair and exquisite creamy skin stand up to this harsh environment?'

Under his intent scrutiny she flushed. "Obviously, you don't think it can be done, or not without consequences. What about your mother?"

"What about her?"

A definite snap. "Not a good subject, right?"

"Sorry," he said. "But my mother, a beautiful woman, by the way—she got all the looks in the Erskine family—had to be the world's worst mother. No, hang on," he said as though seriously considering, "maybe Jan."

She turned her head to face his handsome, hard-edged profile, more than ready to take him to task. "Now that's unkind. *Very* unkind."

"I never claimed to be *kind*," he said and gave her a slight smile. A sexy smile, damn him, but he wasn't getting off the hook.

"Yet you've been kind to me," she pointed out crisply. "Amazingly kind."

"Perhaps I have an ulterior motive?"

"Aah!" She let her bright head fall back. "Why didn't you tell me you wanted an unpaid nanny?"

He let his impatience show. "Surely you're getting free board?" He let his challenging tone hang between them for a second or two. "Don't be ridiculous. I invited you here to enjoy yourself, see our Outback, maybe derive inspiration for your forthcoming blockbuster, and don't you forget it."

"I was only joking."

He took another moment to consider. "No, you weren't."

"Heck, Cal, are we going to fall out on our very first day?" she asked wryly.

His deep laugh, like a chuckle, caught her by surprise. "Amber, you're not supposed to say silly things like that. I had no idea little Marcus would take to you like you were his appointed guardian angel. We had two good women with lots of experience to help and advise Jan. Like I told you, she drove them away with her flash bang verbal breakouts. They took it as long as they could, then literally flew off. Jan doesn't have mood-swings, like Eliot once said. She's in a filthy mood *all* the time. She takes no pleasure or interest in anything. She gives my uncle a really bad time."

Amber had seen enough of Jan's behaviour to well believe it. Still, she felt compelled to stick up for a deeply depressed new mother. This could and did happen to the best of women. "But surely these are symptoms of PND?" she challenged more disapprovingly than she intended. "The appearance of being out of control, the inability to cope with her baby. Jan's to be pitied. She's to be helped. The condition can be quite severe."

"And you think I'm blaming Jan for what she can't control?" He threw her a hard, impatient look.

"Yes." Amber nodded emphatically. The first time she'd laid eyes on him she'd thought he was the kind of man who'd have difficulty in getting in touch with his feminine side.

"And that's a snap analysis?" was his sarcastic rejoinder.

"I'm only saying what I believe. I'm a woman, after all."

"And I haven't noticed?" The green eyes whipped over her, increasing her heart rate. "The thing is, Ms Wyatt—"

"Yes, Mr MacFarlane?" She feigned strict attention.

"The thing is, Amber, we've all lived with it for months now. We thought things would gradually get better. Everyone has been kind and supportive, believe it or not. Even tough old me. I can see you've already labelled me a hard-hearted man. No, don't begin to deny it."

"I wasn't going to," she said sweetly. "It's just that you can't know what it's really like."

"So what do you suggest? I rush out and father a child. See how I go?"

"You'll find out eventually," she pointed out calmly. "I didn't say I don't think you'd make a good dad."

"But your preference is for sensitive New Age guys," he mocked. "I won't at this point mention that wimp, Sinclair. It defies logic that a woman as intelligent as you dedicated herself to such a louse. How the hell did that happen?"

She gulped in air. "Hey, might I remind you you're not my keeper? Anyway, you're not the one to talk."

"Of course I'm not," he agreed. "Maybe one day they'll isolate the hormone that causes physical attraction."

"You're suggesting they find the antidote? Believe me, it won't work."

"Well, we can save that for another time. There's nothing to be gained from mooning about the past."

"Who's mooning?" she sweetly asked.

"You said that as if you meant it."

"I do. What about you?"

"I do the best I can." He gave her a sideways grin. "As for Janis, Eliot has had loads—and I mean *loads*—of her favourite flowers flown in. The most expensive flowers ever packed up by a florist, I guarantee. They cost oodles! The bill put even me into shock. Anyway, why don't we get off the subject of Jan?" He knew he sounded a little harsh.

"Her problems won't go away. I do hope Marcus sleeps for your uncle."

"Poor little scrap is suffering pretty severe sleep deprivation," he said, his tone miraculously becoming gentler.

So it was the mother. Not the child. "I just want to say this."

He gave a knowing smile. "Course you do. The investigative journalist. Prize-winning to boot."

She ignored the taunt. "Mrs MacFarlane could be feeling very guilty. She could be feeling shame she can't handle her own baby. She could even be feeling worthless. Have you taken that into account?"

"Would you like to know?" He swerved to avoid an all but hidden boulder, causing the four-wheel drive to rock.

"Of course I would." She straightened up, slightly dizzy with their close proximity. He was *such* a physical man. "I'm asking."

"*You* have taken into account *I'm* not the husband. I'm not the father. I am what I am. Fed up to the back teeth and, before you take me further to task, a very experienced nursing sister from the Royal Flying Doctor team told me privately on her last visit she very much doubted Jan was suffering genuine PND."

"Go on." She turned to him.

"I intend to. Sister Ryan is very familiar with the condition. She advises many young mothers rearing their babies in our Outback isolation."

Amber blew a stray coppery-red lock off her brow. "Okay, so maybe I'm out of line here."

"Don't let *that* bother you," he said dryly. "That's how we met, remember? You being out of line."

"You know, maybe I shouldn't have come out here. Why don't you just tell me to leave?"

He laughed out loud. It was a great sound. "Asking you to leave wouldn't come easily to me. I *like* you, Amber." His eyes sparkled over her. "You're a woman without inhibitions."

"I wouldn't count on that!" She gave him a very speaking glance, at the same moment she felt the imprint of his kisses on her mouth. "Even I, a woman without inhibitions, dare not ask if your uncle's marriage isn't working out. You may well bite my head off. There is the age difference, but it's not all that great. Your uncle is a handsome, very gentlemanly man."

"He's that." The Cattle Baron sighed deeply. "Sometimes it doesn't work with women."

"And no doubt you're a good judge?" Just being with him was giving her a mad rush of exhilaration. Both of them were dealing with old wounds and, maybe now, a resurgence of hormones, chemicals, whatever. The Cattle Baron was man-handling her poor broken heart, though right now she had to question the depth of what she and Sean actually had *had*.

"No better than you, Amber," he said, throwing her another narrow sidelong glance.

That hit a nerve, as it was meant to. "You mean we've both made serious mistakes in the romance stakes," she retaliated.

"Partners in error, you might say. Hindsight has made me think myself a fool."

"And that wouldn't come easily to you. Never mind. Next time we have to lift our standards," she told him briskly.

"Next time?" His vibrant voice positively rasped.

"No need to yell. You're not going to throw me out, are you? I wouldn't like to have to set out on foot."

"You wouldn't get far," he said, laughing.

"So *you* say. Don't underrate me."

"Never!" As a matter of fact, he was half convinced she'd make it.

"I've been in dangerous spots before. Once in Thailand—" She broke off, stunned by the sight that swam into her line of vision. "What in the blue blazes is that? A komodo dragon?" A gigantic lizard, taller than a tall man, was standing on its hind legs and tail, calmly surveying their progress. Its skin, she saw in near horror, was black, strikingly marked with yellow spots. It looked almost as terrifying as a croc.

"That, Ms Wyatt, is a perentie, second only to the komodo dragon in size."

"Thank you, that's quite big enough." She shuddered. "It must be well over six feet."

"Six and a half. That's Yuku. Actually, you're very lucky to see him. Possibly you deserved such a treat. Spotting him isn't all that common. Especially first time out."

"So I've been blessed?"

"Yep." He smiled and her heart twisted that little bit more. In his own way, the Cattle Baron was dynamite. Not an easy man. Not at all. Not overly sympathetic, either. At least to his uncle's wife. She was troubled by that. Frankly, she was trying to find flaws in the superhero.

"You know, this is quite an experience for a city born, city bred girl," she confided. "I'm finding it all very intoxicating."

"Me included?"

"Nope," she answered briskly. "I need to keep my wits about me. I wouldn't like to be out for a stroll and run into Yuku. What does the name mean? No, don't tell me. Aboriginal for Godzilla. You may not be around to protect me."

"And you couldn't outrun him," he pointed out. "Stand perfectly still. But don't worry, Amber. I'll keep an eye on you."

And lead me where? "That's good to know. It must be an extraordinary feeling, knowing you're master of all this." With her hand she indicated the infinite open plains. "I never expected the landscape to be so *dramatic*, or so awe-inspiring. I love all the dry ochre colours. The mirage must be an endless source of fascination, the way it dances and throws up such extraordinary effects. I have to thank you, yet again, for inviting me out here. For the first time in my life, I'm filled with the sense I'm in the *authentic* Australia."

His lean hand reached out, fingers drumming a brief tattoo on her shoulder. "And so you are." He could see her interest in everything she saw, everything she said, was totally unfeigned. He had given her an opportunity and it looked as if she was determined to take full advantage of it. That pleased him more than he cared to acknowledge. Ms Amber Wyatt was rewarding company. "You're in the land of the great explorers," he said. "The overlanders, the incredible brave pioneers, my own ancestors among them, who started up their huge cattle and sheep runs. They built their Outback castles and kept themselves, their families, their employees, stockmen and station hands, and their vast herds and flocks alive."

She could hear the pride in his voice. "And it's a grand achievement to carve out a cattle kingdom in the wilderness."

That afternoon the Cattle Baron showed her life on a great Outback station. They parked on a rocky escarpment that glowed an unbelievable orange with charcoal and sapphire striations. The whole area was littered with curious white stones. Below them a mob of mixed steers, bullocks, cows and calves were being watered at a stream. The trample of so many hooves had churned the water to a rusty red. To Amber's eyes, the cattle looked to be in prime condition. Stockmen on horseback, battered Akubras pulled down low on their foreheads, quietly sat in the saddle, watching on. Moments later, one of the men began to head a number of beasts away from the water. Obviously they had had enough to drink because they went without urging, trotting sedately up the bank, with the stockman harmlessly wielding a whip in the air. The men were all, so far as she could see, aboriginal or part aboriginal. Outback stations would owe a great vote of thanks to their indigenous workforce, she thought, which led her to believe that Mrs MacFarlane was making a huge mistake in not utilizing the skills of Dee's house girls with baby Marcus. The one who had waited at lunch, young Mina, looked as if she would be very gentle and caring with the little fellow.

As the afternoon wore on the glare became more intense. Once she was shocked into crying out in panic, *"Look!"* Her hand shot out to grasp his shoulder.

"I'm looking," he answered with a casualness that unnerved her.

"We're going to drive right into a lake. Look. Dead ahead." Her anxiety was mounting to the extent she was braking hard and quite uselessly with her feet.

"Give it a minute and it will disappear."

Just as he predicted, in under thirty seconds the lake disappeared.

"So what was that?' she asked in astonishment. "The mirage?"

"Get used to it. You're going to see it a lot. The mirage is what so cruelly tricked the early explorers time and time again. Tricked many a traveller. Tricked you."

"It sure did!" Amber had no trouble admitting. "It looked so cool and inviting, then again so oddly out of place in the middle of the spinifex. Makes me wonder if I'm going to be able to trust my eyes."

"Borrow mine." He slanted her a smile.

Her whole body received it like some wonderful benediction.

Last on the agenda was a drive through the holding camps, men waving, calling out greetings to the boss. The Cattle Baron was popular with his workforce. "We won't stop today. Just for now, I don't want you agitating the men."

"Agitating the men?" she echoed in disbelief.

"I'm sure none of them has seen a woman like you in their entire life," he explained. "Another time you can meet them."

"Am I supposed to wear camouflage?"

He laughed and let it go.

Several times they forded creeks and branch creeks, the larger stretches of water afloat with waterlilies, magnificent blooms, pink in one place, lotus-blue in another, cream and ivory. How marvellous they would look in a vase! They bumped across a rushing, rock-strewn gully to get to one lagoon in particular, a huge open span of clear crystal water dotted with little islands covered in palms to rival the tropics.

"A good place to swim," the Cattle Baron told her casually. "You've brought a swimsuit?"

"Sorry, I didn't think. How could I when the rush was so great?"

"Never mind. You can always dive in au naturel."

Normally self-assured, she found herself blushing. All over. "I wouldn't consider it, even if I were on my own."

"So what would you be hiding?" He had to laugh at her expression—half embarrassment, half outrage. "It's all right. Take it easy." He was, in fact, mentally contemplating what Ms Wyatt would look like unclothed. Divine. He kept veering from powerful attraction to remanning his barricades and possibly saving himself a good deal of grief.

Head things off at the pass, MacFarlane.

When they arrived back at the homestead, the sun was setting in such splendour that Amber was reluctant to go indoors.

"Let's stay outside for a few minutes," she begged. "I want to celebrate such beauty. You may be used to it but I've never seen a sky so awash with those breathtaking colours—fiery reds, gold, pinks, glorious apricots! And look at the long trails of pale green, silvery-blue and amethyst. How beautiful!"

"It is that," he agreed. Her responses were spontaneous. She really was soaking it all in. The remoteness that was so threatening to a lot of people, Ms Wyatt appeared to be quite comfortable with.

"The intensity of colour seems almost unreal," she was saying, her eyes on the glory of the western sky. "I've witnessed countless beautiful sunsets before, but nothing like this."

"Now that cheers me, Ms Wyatt," he said and he realised he meant it. "But wait until you see the stars tonight. No city pollution. I can guarantee you'll never have seen a clearer Southern Cross."

How could he miss the heat reflected in her cheeks? If a man had sexual radiance it was he! Exposed to it at such close quarters, it was dazzling.

Inside the great house, peace reigned. The Cattle Baron looked at her with a wry grin. "The world needs more women like you, Ms Wyatt."

"Let's see what's happening first." Amber walked briskly into the informal living area where they had left Eliot MacFarlane and his baby son. Eliot had disappeared but, seated in the armchair, a tender smile on her face, one small brown sandal-shod foot rocking the bouncinette, was Mina. Baby Marcus was wide awake, staring up into Mina's gentle face.

As soon as Mina realised that Mr MacFarlane and his visitor—a bright spirit being, Mina thought—were behind her she jumped up, trembling, out of the chair, a look of guilt on her face. "Dee give me permission," she wailed. "I would never hurt the baby. *Never.* I have little brothers and sisters of me own."

The Cattle Baron held up a hand. "Mina, we would never think for a moment you would harm the baby. Whatever gave you that idea?"

Mina shot a look from the Cattle Baron to Amber, who

smiled reassuringly at her. "Missus Eliot don't want me anywhere near baby."

"That's because she doesn't understand how good and reliable you are, Mina," Cal said, a vertical frown between his strongly marked brows. "You can go now. And thank you. What happened to Mr Eliot, by the way?"

Mina relaxed into a big smile. "Mr Eliot, he fell fast asleep with baby. Dee told him to go an' have a good lie down."

"Thank you, Mina," Cal said. After Mina had hurried off, he turned his attention back to Amber. "So what now?"

"Looks like we're in charge," she said a little wryly.

"Eliot should never have pegged Janis for a full-time mum. He made a bad decision there."

"Now don't go losing your jolly mood." She bent to free baby Marcus from the bouncinette, swooping him into her arms. "Hello, sweetheart. How's it going?"

"I'm sure he can't talk as yet."

"Do *you* want to hold him?" she asked pointedly.

"This is blackmail, Ms Wyatt."

"You know, you need to get more in touch with your tender side." She gave him a challenging look. "Take a crash course in how to handle babies. This is your little cousin. Say hello, Marcus. This is Cousin Cal, the big-shot Cattle Baron."

"Please do *not* condescend, Ms Wyatt. You're entirely at my mercy."

The man could conjure up body heat at a glance. "I'm only having a joke." She really felt that adrenalin jolt.

"You joke a lot."

"What makes you think it's not a good idea? God forbid I should make you angry. Look, Marcus is smiling." Her tone carried surprise and delight.

"Wind?" he suggested, mock polite.

"Marcus is *smiling*," she repeated.

"So he is!" He came in close, an electric presence, letting the baby take hold of his finger. "You're an angel, Ms Wyatt."

"I'm not an angel." She was thrilled with the way Marcus and his powerful cousin were connecting. The gentleness of the Cattle Baron's smile startled her. Maybe he had a lot of heart, after all.

Then he messed up. "I know you're not," he said crisply. "But you are pretty darn special."

"Well, thanks for that."

"It's the least I can say." He bent nearer to the baby. "He's looking at us like *we're* the proud parents." Marcus was still tightly gripping his finger.

"I've been struck by the same thought. You want kids?"

He gave her a long, cool, slow look. "Did I say I wanted kids?"

"Who then shall inherit your kingdom? Seriously now, who? You must want kids. You *need* kids. You wouldn't want me to think otherwise, would you?"

"What if I confess I'm scared of women?"

"You're not scared of me."

"I swear to God I am."

At the devilry in his eyes, every pulse in Amber's body ignited. It was as if she had swallowed a firecracker. "See how contented he is." She lowered her head quickly. "I wonder when he had his last bottle. He's not breastfed?"

"Hell, what a question!' He gave her a look that was positively unnerved for a superhero. "Not my place to go into the details."

"Just thought I'd run it by you."

"Well, I have no idea. I keep right out of the way with that stuff. Anyway, he loves your hair."

"The bright colour." She bent and kissed the top of the baby's head. "At which point do we find out?"

"About what?" Myriad expressions flitted across his dynamic face.

"Don't snap. There *are* limits to my tolerance. And, just to get the record straight, I don't intend to free up time for an affair."

"You wish!" he said witheringly.

Her golden eyes sparkled. "Such arrogance!"

"You'd do well to remember. Anyway, don't let's upset the baby." He turned his dark head as footsteps sounded on the marble floor, which was inlaid with a grid of rosewood, in the central hall. "Here's Dee," he said. "I'm sure she can answer all your questions."

"Got it! But I don't have to like it."

"Meaning what?" He shot her a glance. "No, don't bother. You're finding it too easy to push my buttons. Now I have to go. I have a hundred and one things I need to attend to."

"Well, you're halfway to your office." She gave him a sweet smile. "And thank you once again for your time."

"My pleasure." He gave an exaggerated suave bow.

CHAPTER SEVEN

THEY all came together for dinner. In the interim, with Dee looking on, offering helpful suggestions, Amber had managed to bathe Marcus and give him his bottle—no, he wasn't breast-fed, Mrs MacFarlane hadn't considered it an option. Next, she'd settled him once again in his bouncinette, where he'd immediately returned quite happily to napping.

"The poor little soul is catching up on a whole lot of lost sleep," said Dee. "He's had the roughest time of the lot."

"Let's hope he's coming out of it." Amber was grateful that she and Dee were getting on so well. "It could be time. Some little ones don't settle for a few months, then overnight they're okay."

"You hope! Ya know Mrs MacFarlane is her own worst enemy," Dee half covered her mouth as she said it, as though Janis might be right behind her. "I suppose the poor girl can't help her nature."

"It's sad if she feels inadequate for the task." Amber was still not persuaded that Janis MacFarlane wasn't a victim of PND.

But Dee harrumphed. "She's confident enough to tell everyone off."

"Maybe it's the isolation," Amber suggested. "No support and no contact from another woman from her own family. Her mother."

"I think she has a very poor relationship with her mother," Dee said, folding and refolding a clean bib. "Don't tell her I sent young Mina to mind the child. That'll set her off."

"Surely Eliot would tell her?" Amber's eyes widened. "Why can't he make her see she needs all the help she can get? Mina is only too willing to mind the baby."

"Little thing wouldn't hurt a fly and she's utterly trustworthy," Dee said, very loyal to her staff. "All my girls are. I train them. They pay close attention. They were all born on the station. Went to the station school. They're happiest here. This is *their* country. But it's like I told you, Mrs MacFarlane has…issues."

"Now that *is* sad," Amber said, her voice quiet. "Maybe she needs a little time to adjust to Outback life."

"Maybe." Dee's sceptical response hung in the air. "Might help if she tried to put on a happy face now and again. Not that I'd recognise it if I saw it. The lady has never wasted her charm on me. Unlike others," she added cryptically. "I've seen a lot of people come and go, Amber. You either love the Outback—take to it like a whistling duck to a lagoon—or you never adapt. Cal's mum didn't, though a fair amount of time went by before she lit out. She loved her husband. Not that Jeff Rankin. Never married him anyway. She *adored* her son. I know he won't have it, but she *did*. Big mess up there. Cal's mum couldn't cope with the life. Got to feel like a prisoner. City girl, ya see!"

"Like me," Amber had to point out.

"*Not* like you." Dee gave a quick shake of the head. "You came in from your trip with your eyes shinin'"

"That's a good sign?"

"The best sign there is!" Dee pronounced, patting Amber's arm.

What to wear? The homestead was so splendid, the MacFarlanes so clearly used to the best, she picked out a dress she thought appropriate—a silk maxi. She could have worn it to a garden party. It had lovely full-blown roses, apricot, pink and yellow, printed on a white ground. She'd loved the fabric the minute she'd seen it. It swished delightfully around her ankles. She hoped Janis MacFarlane would join them. She wanted to get her own take on what was so badly troubling the woman. Restored to well-being, Janis MacFarlane could be beautiful. She had to take into account that trained professionals had ruled out PND as the cause of Janis MacFarlane's distress. She wanted her own view. Offer support if permitted. Janis hadn't come forward to object to her bathing and feeding baby Marcus, at any rate.

They dined in yet another area on the east side of the house—a stone colonnaded terrace with a series of arches extending the full length of the rear exterior. The floor was tiled in mosaic form, turquoise, white and orange lifting the deep terracotta. A monumental hewn timber table was beautifully set, the table surrounded by the traditional heavy wicker chairs of South East Asia. It was a wonderfully inviting setting, very cool, lit by many hanging brass lanterns. Amber was able to look out and enjoy a section of the garden which was densely planted with bougainvilleas that thrived in the dry. They spilled and climbed everywhere—pink, orange, bronze and a lovely deep violet. The long flowering bracts simply blazed in the lights.

Rolling the stem of her crystal wineglass between her two fingers, Amber watched the interaction of the family. The Cattle Baron looked marvelous, she thought, realising she was now admiring his style of looks—the strong distinctive features, the taut toughness and his great body. The man fitted his setting. He was simply dressed but high quality all the way—white cotton shirt very up to the moment, safari style, buttoned down pockets, open-necked, over perfectly fitted

khaki-coloured trousers. In the middle of the desert he didn't
need anyone to give him any style tips. His uncle was his
elegant self in a cotton striped shirt and charcoal trousers to
match one of the stripes. Janis MacFarlane looked a great deal
better than the first time Amber had seen her. She wore a
scarlet dress of surprisingly bold cut. The neckline dipped pre-
cariously low. Amber supposed it was because of weight loss.
She wasn't wearing a bra. Her long dark hair was arranged in
an elegant knot, large dark eyes shining. Or was that more a
feverish glint? Amber could see when she was well and happy
how Janis would have dazzled her husband. Her long nails
were painted the same colour as her dress. No housework to
break them. No catching of nails in baby's nappy. She wore
no jewellery around her delicate neck, but the central diamond
in her engagement ring was so big it was a wonder she could
lift her fork.

And she was inexcusably rude. After the initial head to toe
inspection of Amber's person, she rarely looked at her again. She
looked—not at her husband—but, for God's sake at the *Cattle
Baron*. In fact Amber realised with some surprise that she talked
almost exclusively to him. Once her finger reached out and
touched his hand where it lay on the linen and lace table mat.

Dear God!

Amber was shocked into giving a gasp, which she hurriedly
turned into a cough. With utter dismay, she perceived the truth
as if it were all spelt out for her in neon letters ten feet high.

Janis MacFarlane is in love with The Cattle Baron.

How was that for a scenario? It smacked of madness. Worse,
danger. No wonder the woman wasn't functioning properly.

Did Cal know? Did his uncle know? Did Dee know? Surely
Dee had dropped a hint to fuel her perceptions?

A hard lump lodged in Amber's chest. She thought it would
take ages before the shock waves wore off. Janis MacFarlane's
high levels of anger and bitter resentment directed towards her

husband and baby were symptoms not of PND but of being caught in a taboo situation. She had flipped the switch herself. Loving the wrong man would be akin to desolation. Eliot MacFarlane was a fine-looking man, gentle, cultured, but, seen side by side with his nephew, with his youth and blazing aura, his immense sexual radiance, Eliot's attractions all but faded away.

Was that disaster?

Was it ever!

Cal turned his dark head to give her an odd look. "You okay?"

With her head full of horror, she fetched up a smile. "Never better!" She was uncertain now whether her compassion for Janis MacFarlane was lessening or growing. What a penance, falling in love with your husband's nephew!

"So what's your opinion of Jingala beef?" he asked, unaware of Amber's train of thought.

Dee, who was revealing herself as a great cook, had roasted a prime fillet of beef served with a red wine sauce and cooked-to-perfection buttered vegetables.

"Mouth-watering," she said. She'd been hungry when the meal had arrived but the latest revelation had killed her appetite stone dead.

"You can have another glass of shiraz for that." He smiled.

"I hear you lost your job, Ms Wyatt." Janis suddenly spoke up. Her words seemed to carry an odd sting. Amber had the bizarre thought that Janis MacFarlane was jealous of her very presence. Or was she a naturally nasty person? You couldn't just fake PND. One might have to look elsewhere for a cause.

And now Amber knew *where*.

"Give us a break, Jan," Cal groaned. "Amber asked you to use her first name as soon as she walked in."

"Amber, of course." Janis MacFarlane's scarlet mouth pouted. "So sorry. If you were after seclusion…Amber, you couldn't do better than here."

"Then I have to say I love seclusion." Amber caught the Cattle Baron's glittering eyes.

"What?" Janis exclaimed. "You love the vast empty spaces—well, of course you love the homestead—" this delivered very dryly "—or is it the diplomatic thing to say?"

"You don't believe me?" Amber smiled, though it took quite an effort. "But tell me. How did you know I'd lost my job?" Had Cal told her? What *else* had he told her? She hoped she looked cool. She didn't feel cool. In fact, she was beginning to steam up.

"Janis didn't get it from me," the Cattle Baron intervened as though he'd read Amber's mind.

Janis MacFarlane threw back the rest of her wine. She had eaten very, very sparingly but the beautiful wines on offer were quite a different matter. "You're not a complete unknown... Amber," she said, making an unsuccessful attempt at sounding friendly. "Even in the wilds, with the satellite, it's very easy to trace faces and names."

A moment of stunned silence. "You *traced* her?" Cal asked before Amber had a chance to.

"Why, yes! I recognised Amber's face right off. Naturally, I was interested in her story. And does she *have* one!"

"Run it by us," Cal invited, again beating a simmering Amber to a retort. Unless she was growing super-sensitive, Janis MacFarlane's tone wasn't far from open contempt. *Calm down, dammit. Don't let this very odd woman get under your skin.*

"I swear I would have done the same thing in your place, Amber," Janis now assured her. "In fact, I would have been lying in wait for him somewhere."

"Not with a gun, I hope?" This time Amber beat the Cattle Baron off. She was beginning to think Janis MacFarlane well capable of pulling a trigger.

Janis shrugged a thin ivory shoulder. "He deserved punishment for what he did to you. I suppose you still love him?"

Once more the Cattle Baron opened his mouth to reply, presumably on Amber's behalf, but she turned to him sweetly.

"May I speak, please?"

His mouth twitched. "Go right ahead."

"Without interruption?"

His eyes sparkled. "Be my guest."

"Thank you." Amber shifted her gaze to Janis MacFarlane's face. It was openly hostile at this quick exchange between Cal and his guest. More signs of jealousy here? Amber would have been pleased to know that she, on the other hand, looked completely unperturbed. "I really don't know if I ever did love him, Janis," she said. "That's the truest answer I can give. At any rate, I'm not having any vulnerable moments. I'm not spending any time thinking about him. He's married. I doubt I'll speak to him again."

"And I don't blame you." Janis spoke darkly, as though she abandoned men every day. "It's a miracle you've survived so much public humiliation. But you, Cal—" she turned eyes huge with concern on him "—you've risked a lot, haven't you, upsetting your grandfather?"

The Cattle Baron let his irritation show. It caused his uncle to take belated action. It obviously took time for Eliot to marshal his thoughts, Amber mused, not without sympathy. After a blissful first marriage that had ended in tragedy, Eliot appeared to have no real idea what this young woman he had married in such a hurry was on about. Either way, it was up to him to put a stop to her treating him like dirt.

Eliot pressed down on his wife's fingers. "Why are you talking about this, Jan, and at dinner? All of us want a pleasant evening. Cal is his own man. He has never kowtowed to his grandfather. No MacFarlane would. The very last thing we want to do is upset Amber, our guest, never mind Clive Erskine."

"May I have my fingers back?" Janis MacFarlane snapped.

"You're hurting me." She snatched her hand away, looking martyred. "I was just worried about Cal. That's all."

Somehow they got through coffee. At any rate, Janis didn't speak to Amber again. Afterwards, Cal suggested Amber might like a stroll around the home compound before bed.

With that, Janis gave her husband the sharp order. "On your feet, Eliot. I too would like some fresh air."

Eliot's answer was surprisingly tranquil. He looked around the outdoor setting. "I would have thought we were getting plenty. I think we'd do a whole lot better looking in on our son."

Right on!

Outside, under the gloriously blossoming stars, Amber started to unwind. "Gosh, does Janis ever have a good day?"

"She could well do," Cal replied after a moment's consideration. "It's just I haven't seen it. Eliot isn't terribly good at pulling her into line either."

"How *does* one pull a woman into line?" Amber asked, wondering how the Cattle Baron would go about it.

"You sound like you'd expect me to break teeth?"

"Is that an answer?" she said, laughing.

"You're not getting a rise out of me, Amber," he told her dryly.

"Okay, let's regroup. Tell me about the stars. You're absolutely right. I've never seen anything to equal the numbers, the size and the brilliance. The Southern Cross has never looked so bright or so close, or the Milky Way so luminous." She lifted her head in a gesture of worship to the great dazzling vault of the sky, spanned by millions of twinkling, sparkling stars. "The aboriginal people have all sorts of myths and legends about the stars, don't they?"

"Sun, moon and stars. Every living thing, every mystery explained. The Milky Way is the home of the great beings. It's also our home if we've lived a good life. Of course the myths vary from region to region. One of the most interesting facets of mythology is ritual. The two complement each other. I'll speak to one of our tribal elders, Jimmy Possum, about organising a corroboree for you, one that's not sacred—"

"Before I go?" She was unwilling to explore her burgeoning feelings about the Cattle Baron, but she had to admit that he had gained powerful entry into her life.

"Do you *want* to go?" He looked down on her from his superior height.

"Not for ages! This is the most exciting adventure I've had in my life."

"And you're barely into it," he answered suavely.

"Listen, I *meant* it." The challenge in his manner kept her on a knife edge. "You have major trust issues with women, don't you?" she ventured. "What do you actually *need* from a woman to trust her?" She allowed him to take her arm to draw her away from an overhanging frond. If she had been carrying something she would have dropped it, so nerveless did he render her limbs.

"You think that's my problem?" He released her, taking his time.

"Like me, your fiancée betrayed you. That's got to hurt!" She shook her head with real feeling, the movement making the deep sinuous waves of her hair bounce.

"Hurt at the time, but betrayal is part of a man's education," he returned in a clipped voice.

"Don't forget us girls."

"I doubt if I could forget *you*, Ms Wyatt." He gave a mocking sigh of admiration.

"You ticked Janis off for calling me Ms Wyatt."

"The problem with Janis is that, unlike me, she wasn't doing it in fun."

"So it's fun, is it?"

"We both know it is."

She did know. Had it been another two people, she would have said they were flirting. Silly word. The Cattle Baron was above and beyond flirting. So was she, for that matter. "So what about a few legends?" Here, in the perfumed semi-dark, excitement was picking up at an alarming rate. The man's aura of sexuality had a tremendous edge.

"I'm weighing up which ones to tell you," he said. "Some of them are pretty damned erotic."

"Like the tales of the Arabian Nights?"

"Are you telling me you've read them?" he asked with a catch of laughter in his voice.

"Actually, when I was a kid I got hold of an old copy. I used to read everything and anything I could get my hands on. I remember it was in a trunk with lots of other old books. I couldn't make head or tail of it, but it sure beat a comic book."

"I should hope you couldn't understand it, not if you were a child. Anyway, I'm sure you've caught up over the years. Did you and Sinclair live together?"

"No, we didn't!" she said crossly. "I guess I had that much sense. Anyway, I've warned you. Let's forget about him unless you want us to have a heart to heart about your ex."

"Brooke is history."

"So *you* say. You never run into her?"

He extended a long arm to hold up another frond overhanging the pathway. "Not often when so many miles separate us."

"So where does she live? As the crow flies?"

"You can go on the Internet and find out all about her family," he said. "Her father is Peter Rowlands. They're an old pastoral family. It would seem the Internet is Jan's only form of relaxation. The Rowlands' flagship station, Goorack, is about one hundred and fifty miles north-east of here."

"Impressive?"

"Well, it's not right up there with Jingala, Kinjarra, Daramba and the like, but impressive enough," he said.

"Did you ever give her a chance to say she was sorry?" She felt compelled to know.

"Ms Wyatt, as far as I'm concerned, being unfaithful wraps the whole thing up."

"So that's a no, then?"

"Well, I won't screw up and appear at her wedding."

"Couldn't resist it, could you?" she said in disgust. "Your ex is getting married?"

"Not as far as I know." The reply was bland.

"Oh, that is so like you!" Her tone was laced with irritation.

"But you don't have any real idea what I'm like, Amber Wyatt. For instance, did you know I'm dying to kiss you?"

She had to brace herself against the shock. The man had sex appeal on tap. "One way of shutting me up?"

"You know what they say. The only way to get rid of temptation is to yield to it."

"Oscar Wilde." She sucked in a breath as his hands dropped to her waist. "What's going on here, Cal?"

"Just a kiss in the dark," he said smoothly. "All part of your Outback adventure. We can revert to our normal selves the minute we go back inside."

His handsome face was very close, his male charisma scattering her defences to the desert winds. "Look, the last thing I should do is encourage you." She braced her hands against his hard muscled chest.

"Sure about that?"

"Spare me the arrogance, Cal MacFarlane."

"Not arrogance. Think of it as therapy. For both of us and our wounded hearts. Neither of us is looking for a long-term involvement right now, are we? Our lifestyles are totally incompatible and so forth. Going on our past experience, a shared kiss would be a very pleasant way to round off the evening."

"I don't know if pleasant is the right word. A bit tame in

comparison to our last encounter. But then both of us were het up at the time. Right now, I think it best if I pull away."

"Why don't you?"

"You may well ask. It's not easy." She laughed. She was still laughing when he covered her mouth with a low murmur that sounded very much like yearning.

Whatever, she lost it.

Entirely.

How could her body be responding, *rejoicing,* in this way? She had never believed herself to be fickle. And yet she was opening her mouth to him, feeling the warm pressure of his lips, his tongue sliding over her teeth, bringing up her arms to clasp behind his neck, closing her eyes tight with the brilliant stars shining down on her heavy lids.

How long did it last?

She didn't know. The only thing she *did* know was that she hadn't pushed him away. The mouth that covered hers with so much passion and mastery might well have encircled her heart. It was tremendous. It was dizzying. It was also very bewildering. She would have to re-evaluate her whole adult life. It wasn't all that long ago she'd believed her heart to have been slashed to ribbons.

What a turnaround that was! She had sloughed off the old Amber and become a new woman. Maybe a touch demented.

When he finally lifted his head she leaned heavily against him, revelling in his height and his strength. Temporarily she felt unable and unwilling to stand free.

He kissed the top of her head. "I thought when I kissed you at the wedding that no woman could have responded better. Now you've thrown in a little extra."

"That I have! Take it as glorious lunacy. Don't expect *all* my self-control to disappear."

"God knows I'll have to get a handle on my own." There was a mixture of laughter and self-mockery in his tone. "But on no account need you fear I'll overstep the boundaries," he assured her. "Are you able to walk on?"

Her response was a little tart in the face of his mockery. "How many other women have you kissed that swoon?"

"None more thrilling than you," he replied.

"As if I believe you!"

Even so, she seemed to be floating in the perfumed darkness. She had never been more conscious of her own body, of her skin, its largest, most sensitive organ. She might not have been wearing any clothes at all, she felt so exposed to his every glance, let alone the touch of his hand.

"You should."

He sounded serious. "All the more reason to keep the brakes on, surely?" she warned. "Both of us have had our trust smashed."

"More like dented."

She lifted her head. "I thought you loved your ex-fiancée?"

"At one time, so did I. It seems obvious now that I didn't search far enough for the woman I want. Neither did you for the right man."

"When you get right down to it, no," she admitted with a sigh. "But don't let's spoil a beautiful night mulling over our past mistakes. What about a legend or two? As a child I loved stories. My father used to read to me at bedtime. I loved him so much."

"And he would have loved you, his little princess." Again, he surprised her by dropping another kiss on the top of her head. His empathy was genuine. It filled her with warmth and a surprising measure of comfort. "Maybe you don't have your father, Amber, but you have a lot of happy memories."

"He has never really died for me." Her voice broke a little.

"My dad either," he said, so much the man he wasn't afraid to show his feelings. "I still see him around the station." He lifted his dark head, pointing with one hand. "He's up there among the countless millions of stars in the Milky Way. That's where heroes go. There's a story about the Milky Way's creation. What to hear it?"

"I told you. I love legends."

"Well, then…" He took her arm. "Once, during the Dreamtime, there was a giant Being called Ngurunderi who resolved to brighten the night sky…"

Going to sleep was out of the question. She was too wound up. To be honest, too erotically charged. Amber moved around her bedroom in her nightdress, touching this, studying that, unable to relax. Not to put too fine a point on it, she had never felt more stirred up in her life. That was just how good the Cattle Baron was. Out of nowhere an irresistible force had blasted his way into her life. She barely knew him, yet she felt as though he had always been somewhere at the back of her mind. She could still feel the warmth of his skin, the strength of his hands, the male scent of him, the slight rasp of his beard, the wondrous pressure of his mouth on hers. She felt weak even thinking about it. How in the world had his ex-fiancée ever let him go? She had to be mad. Or she had so missed the excitement of the man, the marvellous sex, when he was away, that she had surrendered to a one-night stand for simple relief? Such things happened.

Not apparently to the Cattle Baron. One strike and you're out! Not that she would have taken Sean back, even if he hadn't married his Georgie. She didn't even waste time wondering if they were enjoying their honeymoon.

The other thing that was really worrying her was Janis MacFarlane. Eliot should pack up his wife and child and never come back. Not until his nephew was safely married to someone who wouldn't let another woman in the world steal her man. It must be utter agony for Janis, living under the same roof with an impossible dream. It didn't excuse her lashing out but it did explain a good deal. The biggest victim here was little Marcus. Surely Janis realized that love for her little son could save her? So many women were desperate to have a child—undergoing protracted procedures—yet Janis couldn't see her baby as her most precious possession.

Amber had no answer for that.

Just as she was contemplating turning in, a thundering came on the heavy mahogany door. Those were some tough knuckles! Could the Cattle Baron be so blatant? Not possible. Even if he were, that didn't lower her level of desire.

Swiftly she belted her satin robe tightly around her, thrust her long hair over her shoulder and went to answer before the door was broken down.

"Cal!" Her heart leapt. She couldn't bank it down. "What is this—a very noisy seduction scene first night off?"

"Is that what it looks like?" His green eyes, normally so cool, were ablaze.

"Well…" She hesitated, not sure she could handle this veritable powerhouse of passion, let alone herself.

"Oh, for God's sake, do I look nakedly desirous?" he asked jaggedly.

"I can't pronounce on that with any degree of confidence. Are you?"

"More than you'll ever know," he groaned. Here was this glorious woman, her hair springing back from her radiant creamy face, her slender body just barely hidden by a filmy pink nightdress and a slinky satin robe right there in front of him. Maybe even his for the taking. She would have turned on a monk. She was turning him on right now. But there was an embarrassing crisis to hand. "Janis is having the mother of all tantrums," he explained. "It's the baby I'm worried about. He's screaming. The seduction scene will have to keep for another night. I promise I'll make it worth the wait. For now, we desperately need your calming hands."

She could handle that. "And leave the rest of me behind?" she joked, to bring down the tension.

"Bring the lot."

Her gaze swept over him. He wore a red T-shirt and a pair of jeans he must have hastily pulled on, crow-black curls tousled. She was experiencing a heaviness in the lower part of her body. God, she wanted him...wanted him... An overpowering sexual urge. No need to feel guilty. "Should I dress?"

"I've never seen a woman look better in my life. Come now. Just as you are. Babies shouldn't be allowed to cry like that. Janis just gives in to her moods. I'd say histrionics."

He could well be right. But either way the woman was in pain. Amber couldn't find it in her heart to entirely blame her.

Following in his tempestuous wake, Amber all but flew down the corridor as Cal strode towards the suite of rooms his uncle and Janis occupied, the adjoining sitting room turned temporarily into a nursery. Eliot, white beneath his tan, must have heard Cal's heavy footsteps—he was making no attempt to walk quietly or to keep to the muffling Persian runner—because Eliot opened the bedroom door, dressed in pyjamas covered by a navy silk robe.

"This is not my finest hour," he said.

Amber fancied he was right. Why *did* he let things get so out of hand?

Inside, Janis was standing in the middle of the huge opulent room, yanking at her long hair, her dark eyes the size of saucers. "Who asked her?" she screeched. It was so loud it almost pinned Amber to the door. "I don't want her. What's she doing here?"

No one answered her. Cal strode through to the adjoining

room where the baby was screaming his tiny head off, as well he might. He was back within seconds, making for Amber and handing her the baby. "Boy, I bet he's glad to see you again," he muttered.

"Amber, I'm so sorry," Eliot MacFarlane said. "Much to our relief, Marcus had been sleeping. Then he woke up."

"Screaming his head off as usual, just as I had fallen asleep," Janis MacFarlane complained bitterly, her delicate features drawn tight. "Doesn't *anyone* sympathize with me? It's always the *baby*. What about *me*? Don't I matter?"

Again no one answered. Janis MacFarlane's main concern seemed to be herself. Even then, Amber was reluctant to lay blame. Was she using anger as an antidote to thwarted passion?

"Eliot, doesn't Janis have a tranquilliser?" Cal turned to his uncle, trying very hard to curb his impatience. "She sounds like she's in need of one."

"She's already downed a couple of pills," Eliot told his nephew unhappily.

"Here, let me help you, Janis." Amber settled the baby over her shoulder, swaying gently. "I'll take him outside until he settles down again. I might go down to my bedroom, if that's okay." Exhausted, little Marcus snuggled in to Amber's warm receptive body, the piteous cries banking down to shuddery whimpers and hiccups.

"What *are* you?" Janis was fuelled by an overriding jealousy that had nothing to do with the baby. "A bloody earth mother? I wonder how good you'd be if you had a little monster like this one."

"Ever wonder if it's because you're rejecting him," Cal retorted curtly, unable to help himself. He turned to join Amber. "I'll stay with Marcus if I have to, Eliot. You look terrible. I'm worried about you. Both of you go back to bed. We have to find a solution to this. It's gone on far too long.

The best professional help has been made available to you, Janis, but you've driven everyone away. You have no choice now. I won't abide it."

"God, what a mess!" Cal followed Amber, baby over her shoulder, into her bedroom. "I shouldn't have brought you out here. I apologise a million times. You've been the best!"

"Hush!" she whispered.

Very quietly he approached. The baby's tiny body was rising and falling very gently. His little hand was caught into the glittering mass of Amber's hair. Her robe had fallen open—the satin sash had come loose, dangling in its loops. He could see the exquisite curves of her naked breasts. Never had the sight of a woman and baby moved him so profoundly. No wonder the great artists of the Renaissance had produced masterpiece after masterpiece of Madonna and child. He couldn't help himself. He imagined her nursing *their* child. The thought shocked him, not only with its element of eroticism. It was all he could do not to pull the three of them into bed.

"So what now?" he whispered. "Do you want me to take him?" He was fully prepared to. It struck him how much sympathy he had for this poor little unloved scrap. Unloved by his mother. At least at this point. Would it ever change? Eliot loved his son but it seemed that he had come to fatherhood too late. He certainly couldn't control his wife.

"I think he needs to be close to me for a while," Amber said. "I felt very sorry for Janis and your uncle but Janis does need help. I couldn't help noticing at dinner she hardly ate a bite, as if food was irrelevant. She could be missing out on essential vitamins and minerals."

"All this has been pointed out to her, Amber," he said testily.

"I guess. Why don't you advise them to go away for a while until she's feeling more able to cope? Take a trip."

"And leave Marcus behind?" His black eyebrows shot up.

"Yes," she answered, matching whisper for whisper. "We can get things organised."

"We? God, Amber, there aren't enough hours in the day for me. I have a big station to run. Outstations to visit."

"Don't think I don't admire the level of your dedication."

"So you surely don't expect me to babysit the little chap?"

"Who's asking you to?" She stared into his face, his handsome features drawn tight. There was a pulse throbbing away in his temple. She realised that, one way and another, he had put up with a good deal. This wasn't *his* problem. "Though you might be expected to babysit at some time in the future. Modern dads have to pull their weight."

"Whoa!" He held up his hands. "I take it you mean if and when *I* become a dad?"

She gave him a smile full of unconscious allure. "Come on, you know you want to."

Of course he would! With *her* as his child's mother. The thought just surfaced. "No wonder you're a journalist," he said. "Winkling information out of people."

"I'm taking your measure, Cal MacFarlane."

"And I'm taking yours."

"Don't think I haven't noticed." They were indeed evaluating one another. To what purpose? Forming an intimate bond? Crazy as it was, she was more than willing to give it a go. "If your uncle and Janis are agreeable, Dee and I and young Mina will get baby Marcus into a routine. Janis's unhappiness has been contagious. For the time being, Marcus might settle better without her."

"Have you any idea what you're taking on?" He cast an eye on the child. Marcus had fallen off to sleep again. How had *that* happened? It had to be woman magic. *This* woman's magic. What a God-given asset!

"Of course I do, silly man."

"Silly man?" He gave her a look of pure disbelief. "Excuse me, Ms Wyatt."

"You're a big boy. You can take it. Why don't you go back to bed? Marcus can stay with me for the night."

"Maybe it would be a good idea if I slept on the other side?" There was a sudden sparkle in his green eyes.

"You're joking, of course?"

"Actually, I wouldn't mind." He pinned her with a beautiful wry smile. "I wouldn't mind at all. The bed is big enough to make us all comfortable."

"I'm not going to let you tempt me." And he definitely was. "There's no need to stay. Go now. We'll be fine."

"Why don't I sit down and wait until you're both in bed?" he suggested, not happy at the thought of leaving her alone to cope.

"No, I'm kicking you out now. You're too much of a distraction. See, Marcus is breathing quietly. I'm quiet. He's quiet. I can manage. I'm a babysitter from way back."

"Okay," he agreed reluctantly. "You know I'm building up a big debt to you?"

"Don't worry. I'll see to it you pay up."

"The sooner the better," he said.

It sounded lovely. "Night, night, Cal," she softly called. "Pleasant dreams."

He walked to the door—tall, dark, terrific. "I have a sneaking feeling they'll be about *you*. You're a rare woman, Amber Wyatt."

"Hardly!"

"You're too modest. I, for one, am ready to elevate you to that status."

CHAPTER EIGHT

CAL thought he wouldn't sleep a wink, body and mind so aroused, but he didn't stir until dawn.

One glance at the bedside clock and he leapt out of bed, raced into the shower, afterwards throwing on his everyday gear, all the while his mind filled with the sight of a beautiful copper-haired woman cradling a baby to her breast. What had he been thinking of, inviting her out here with things being what they were? Janis running off the rails, little Marcus crying and wailing non-stop, although *he* didn't have to listen to the crying all day, his uncle rendered near impotent in the face of his wife's total inability to cope—worse, her rejection of all help. Good, caring women had been driven away with Jan screaming after them that she just wanted to be left alone. Yet Amber Wyatt with her beauty, her humour, her grace and compassion had reached out to little Marcus and miraculously found a connection.

But it was only a temporary solution to a big problem. Not all women were nurturers. His own mother had cleared off, but at least she had seen him through a lot of years of his childhood. This post-natal depression thing was a mystery to him. In the beginning everyone had shown the greatest tolerance to the baby's crying and Jan's displays of anger and bitter resentment, but she had rejected all help. It was more like she felt *trapped*. Trapped by motherhood? Trapped by her marriage? He would have said Jan wanted *out* of the whole caboodle. He knew Amber was watching him closely, gauging his reactions, concerned he wasn't showing enough sympathy. Maybe he wasn't. His sympathy lay with Marcus and his uncle. Jan's behaviour was just plain bizarre.

No sound from either wing of the house. Peace reigned. He walked very softly down the corridor, making sure he kept to the Persian runner. He would take the little fellow down to Dee, who was always up early. He would feed the baby himself if he had to. Hell, it couldn't be that hard. And, as Amber had reminded him, he had better get in some practice. Of course he wanted kids. He had planned to have his own happy family for most of his life. Brooke had failed him. He shunned the idea of infidelity. Why wouldn't he? His mother had betrayed him and his father. Were his veins clogged up with mistrust? They had been up to date.

Amber too had had a painful lesson. But she was one gutsy lady. And she was his guest. Not the new nanny. He was seriously embarrassed. Very gently, he tapped on the door, waited. No sound from within. His hand on the brass knob, his body tense, he turned it slowly, opening back the door a fraction, listening all the while.

Dawn was casting a soft pearl-grey light over the room. A single bedside lamp was still burning. Amber lay sleeping with the baby cradled in her arms. Just as in his vision, Marcus lay cuddled up contentedly against her breast, his light cap of dark hair contrasting with this vision in pink, copper, cream and vanilla.

The image was so powerful, so beautiful, he stood transfixed. She hadn't made it into bed. The day bed had made a comfortable resting place for both of them, a light rug serving as a blanket. He had a tremendous urge to kiss Amber's sleeping mouth. It was gently parted on the lightest exhalations.

"Amber?" Unable to stop himself, he bent low over her, brushing her mouth with his own. Even that light pressure made his head swim. Despite his every reservation, he had connected with this woman. He had from the moment he'd laid eyes on her. Something had happened. He knew she felt it too. Something that had confounded them both. Could he allow himself to believe she was the woman to bring him lasting happiness? For that matter, could she believe it of him? Both of them had been hurt by infidelity. Since Amber had moved into his life, he had come to see that Brooke's defection hadn't left lasting scars. They had all but healed up.

She must have been dreaming because she thought Cal had kissed her. A butterfly kiss that nevertheless flew deep inside her. "Oh, my goodness, it's morning," she said, blinking.

"Dawn." He was unsettled by the rush of emotions he was fighting. A mere leaf in a storm. "Let me take him. I can put him down on the bed. Bolster him with pillows."

"I was afraid I'd fall off to sleep and maybe roll on him." She was speaking so softly he barely heard her. "He's so *tiny*."

Very gently, Cal took the sleeping child from her, holding him a while. He was a dear little fellow really. He could see a family resemblance. The eyes were blue, not Jan's dark brown. Why should there be such trauma in life?

Amber stretched her arms first, next her legs. Then she wiggled her toes, trying to get the circulation back into her body. Truth be told, she felt quite groggy. Even on her feet she swayed.

"You okay?" Cal wanted to go to her. The effect she was having on him was gaining an awesome momentum. He had already started to fantasize about her. So what was he going to do about it? Was he ready for another serious commitment? Was she? There were big barriers in the way. He couldn't give up his heritage. It was the woman who would have to come to him. Could Amber turn her back on a glamorous city lifestyle?

The higher a man flies, the bigger the crash, said the voice in his head.

He had built a lot of defensive strategies. She was making rubble of them.

Amber began to plait her hair. "I'm fine. Don't worry. The day bed was quite comfortable. What are you going to do with Marc? I'd like to take a shower to wake myself up."

"Go ahead." God, if only there were no restraints! He'd give anything to join her. Soap his trembling hands. Run them over that beautiful woman's body. Instead, he lay the sleeping baby on the canopied bed. "I'll wait here with him. When you're ready we can go downstairs."

She gave him another one of those smiles that wrapped him like a cloud. With this woman he was going some place he had never been before.

"I'm sure he'll be ready for a bottle by then." Amber grabbed up a few clothes, making for the en-suite bathroom.

"Well, for cryin' out loud!" Dee exclaimed when she caught sight of them. "This is borderin' on a miracle."

"And good morning to you too, Dee," Cal said. "Any chance of breakfast?"

"Don't I always get you breakfast?" She gave him an indulgent smile before glancing quickly at Amber, carrying the baby. "How are *you*, love?"

"Fine, Dee." Amber returned the smile. "Our little man had a good night. As you can see, he's awake now and I'm guessing he wants his bottle."

"Breakfast and a bottle comin' up!" Dee bustled away.

Breakfast over, the Cattle Baron was on his feet to go. "The vet will be flying in around eleven," he informed Dee, throwing his linen napkin down on the table. "We'll give him lunch, Dee, as usual."

"No problem," Dee said, busy stacking plates.

He turned quickly to Amber, who was giving the baby a bottle. Miracle of miracles, Marcus was feeding contentedly. How different was one human being from another? Cal marvelled. "When I've got a minute I'll take you around to the stables and let you pick out a horse," he told her. "I didn't bring you here to—"

"Forget it," she broke in, knowing he was embarrassed by his family situation. "I'm enjoying this. Maybe baby Marcus is getting over his problem. It does happen."

Eliot came down not long after, anxious to give his nephew a hand. Cal was handling far more than could be asked of one man and he had been for some time. Eliot knew it and felt bad. "Fitz" Fitzgerald, the vet, was flying in to make a spot check of the herd. He and Fitz went back a long way. He wanted to be on hand. He and Fitz could make their tour while Cal got on with more pressing matters. The big muster was on before Christmas. Back-breaking, often dangerous work.

Janis didn't appear until around ten and what a world of difference there was between husband and wife! Eliot MacFarlane couldn't have been more courteous, courtly, Amber thought, but Janis freaked out when she saw who was sitting happily minding a wide awake, tranquil baby.

"Get up. Get out of here." Janis zoomed in on the hapless Mina, waving her arms as one might wave at a wallaby that had invaded the home gardens.

"Miss Amber…Miss Amber…" Mina stood cross-legged, looking as if she was about to wet her pants with fright.

"Miss Amber is *no one* around here," Janis exploded furiously. "Is that understood? Haven't I told you never to go near the baby?"

"Yes, Missus." Mina was now in floods of tears.

"Yet you've disobeyed me. I'll see to it you lose your place in the house."

Mina, deeply distressed and frightened, hit herself in the head with both hands.

Amber and Dee, a room away, heard the uproar. "Oh, my God, I'll have to get in there," Amber cried.

"My fault again." Dee hung her head.

"Don't be silly." Amber rushed away, desperate to ease the situation. Janis had no hesitation in taking all the help that was offered while still reserving the right to abuse whomever she liked. Everyone wanted to help her. Didn't she know that? Or was she too self-involved to care?

Mina looked as though she was about to break into a run. The lovely peace had been shattered. Marcus had passed from contentment to distress, his wails gathering strength.

"Is this your doing?" Janis swung on Amber, her cheeks red with rage. "Exactly *who* declared you in charge? How dare you override my orders?"

The articulate Amber swallowed the retort that came to mind. For the moment she had to placate this ill-tempered woman. "Mina, I'd like you to go into the kitchen," she said to the shaking girl. "You've done nothing wrong. Dee will have a cup of tea for you."

"May I ask if you're crazy?" Janis stared at Amber as if she'd taken leave of her senses.

"You may *ask* certainly." Amber recovered her equilibrium fast. She waited calmly for Mina to disappear.

"You come in here, a visitor, and defy me?" Janis was shuddering all over with outrage.

Amber kept her tone low. "Spare me, Mrs MacFarlane. Have you noticed your baby? Are you going to pick up your little son or shall I? Didn't you see when you came in he was quite content. Now he's screaming his head off. Look at him. Really *look*. He's every bit as distressed as you are."

Janis didn't even glance down. "You interfering bitch," she said with great venom. "Wait until I tell Cal about this."

"Why tell Cal anything?" Amber gave the other woman a straight look. "You have your *husband*. Now, are you going to try to settle your little son? Please look at him. He's yours. You brought him into the world."

"And a sorry mistake that was." Janis turned on her heel. "I'm going to find Cal."

Poor deluded woman! "I don't think you'll get a good reception," Amber warned. "You heard him last night. The household is at the end of its tether. Please make an effort to calm down, Mrs MacFarlane. I know it's easier said than done, but *please* try. I'll take Marcus, shall I?" Amber didn't wait for a reply, though none appeared to be forthcoming. She settled the baby over her shoulder, patting his heaving little back, while he sicked up on her cotton shirt. Well, she could change it. "Wait here, will you, Mrs MacFarlane?" she begged. "I'll take Marcus through to Dee. She'll take care of him. I'm sure you don't want his crying to continue."

"And I'm supposed to be *grateful* to you?" Janis's dark eyes flashed.

Definitely, Amber thought. "Mrs MacFarlane, I don't need or expect gratitude but you might learn from me about calming a distressed baby. I'll go now, but I'll be back. Please stay. I want to help you, in case you haven't noticed."

"You think you could?" Janis gave a dry smile.

"I'd like to try."

Although Amber fully expected to find the room empty, Janis MacFarlane was standing rigid, as though cemented in place.

"Why don't we sit down?" Amber suggested as pleasantly as she could. This was one difficult woman. She wondered what a happy Janis would look like. *Was* there a happy Janis? She appeared to be highly strung by nature. Had pregnancy and giving birth exacerbated an underlying psychological problem? Eating might help. Thinking that, she said, "You haven't had anything to eat. What would you like for breakfast? It won't take me a minute to tell Dee."

"Don't bother. I'm not hungry." Janis flopped into an armchair.

"You mightn't feel hungry but it's difficult to function without food. What about fruit juice and cereal or maybe scrambled eggs?"

"Do shut up," Janis said rudely. "When I need your help I'll ask for it. And I *don't* need it. I pegged you for an opportunist the moment I laid eyes on you. What's your connection to Cal?"

Amber wasn't in the least surprised this particular question had surfaced. "None of your business, Mrs MacFarlane."

"Are you sleeping together?" Janis's dark eyes ran all over Amber's body. She looked as though she would have liked to use a cattle prod instead.

"Again, none of your business. You might consider I was fully occupied looking after your baby son, though I didn't catch a thank you. Why do you treat him as though he's not yours? I know a little about post-natal depression. I have great sympathy for women who have to confront and deal with it. It would be extremely difficult to handle without help and support. Why did you send those two nannies away? Had you allowed them to help you, you might be feeling a whole lot better by now."

'That's your half baked opinion, is it?" Janis mocked. "No one can fix me." She said it as if it were the end of the world.

"What's so unfixable?" Amber asked with real sympathy, though she could darn near taste the answer. "You have a child—a son, a priceless gift. You have a husband, a lovely man. Perhaps you'd be happier in your own home?"

Janis snorted. "Trying to get rid of me?"

Leave the coast free? Amber shook her head. "I just thought you might be finding the isolation tough going. A lot of women would. Especially one who has had a successful city career. I had the idea that you and Eliot intended living in Melbourne."

"Here's the problem," Janis said savagely. "Eliot brought me back *here*."

"Are you saying he reneged on his word?" Amber was shocked. Had Eliot deliberately put his wife into a situation she couldn't handle?

"We had a very short courtship." Janis presented a bitter face. "I never met Cal until the day of the wedding."

Here it was. Cause and effect. Janis meets Cal. Janis is instantly infatuated with Cal. Husband and baby bear the brunt of wife and mother's unrequited love.

Janis stood up abruptly, angry she might have given an insight into her real problem. "I've endured your company as long as I can, Ms Wyatt. You're nothing more than an ambitious hustler, even if you are beautiful in a way I don't admire. If you're hoping to land Cal, you'd better think again. He and Brooke Rowlands have a *long* history. Brooke may have stuffed up but she's looking for an opening to get back into his good graces. Very persistent lady is Brooke. Once she finds out *you're* here, she'll come calling. Mark my words."

"Sorry, is that supposed to affect me?" Amber sat back, a model of calm outside, upset within. "It doesn't. I understood from Cal that Ms Rowlands isn't all that welcome." How she was succeeding in maintaining a level tone, Amber didn't know. She put it down to her training and withstanding the likes of Jack Matthews.

"That's what he *says*!" Janis pronounced bitterly, as though no man on earth was to be trusted. "The last time she stayed—which wasn't all that long ago—she managed to share his bed. There, shocked you, didn't I?"

"You look more shocked than I do," Amber pointed out quietly, even though the woman was right. She *was* shocked.

"If I were you, Mrs MacFarlane, I'd start counting my blessings. The closest man in the world to you is your *husband*. Your most precious possession is your baby son. If you keep that in mind, you might start to feel better. By the way, unless you intend to take over the management of Marcus, you'll allow me, Dee and young Mina, who is the gentlest little soul in the world, to give you a hand. I can see Cal's opinion is important to you. You must realise Cal has had enough of your issues with the staff."

"Oh, how splendid!" Janis clapped her hands. "A crusader for staff rights!"

"Unlike you," Amber returned quietly.

Janis MacFarlane gave her a furious stare. "And you can go to hell, Ms Wyatt. I begin to see why your fiancé dropped you for the Erskine girl. This conversation is over. It bores me. I'm going to get a little air." She headed towards the front door, mistress to servant.

"Doesn't that leave us holding the baby?" Amber called ironically. The woman's failure to assume responsibility was incomprehensible. Janis MacFarlane appeared to have written her baby off, as though he didn't exist.

Now she swung back with such a strange smile that Amber's heart sank. "You can have him if you want him," she said.

Could there be anything worse than that?

Cal and Eliot came back at lunchtime with their regular vet, an amiable man with a mop of sandy hair that might at one stage have been ginger, the countless freckles his skin had thrown up for protection forming a pseudo tan. Pleasant though he was, he nevertheless managed to stir the cauldron by asking Janis, albeit very kindly, if she was getting on any better with her baby.

Janis let her face show her extreme resentment. "I'm beginning to think he should be taken into care until he settles," she said as though she had just come up with the solution to her problems. "That's if he *ever* does."

"But of course he will, poor little fella!" Fitz Fitzgerald, grandfather of eight, protested, staring from Eliot to his young wife in astonishment. "Where is he now?"

"Ask Ms Wyatt," Janis suggested tightly. "She seems to have taken over the running of the household."

Beneath the starched white tablecloth Amber clamped her hand down hard on the Cattle Baron's knee. She knew he was longing to intervene. But she could fight her own battles. She offered the vet a smile. "Marcus is coming along just fine. Mina is watching him at the moment. She's good with children. She has little brothers and sisters."

Janis's cheeks flushed as she spluttered, "This is not *my* idea, Mr Fitzgerald. Next thing we know, Ms Wyatt will have the girl taking Marcus walkabout."

"I think we'll take it more gradually than that, Janis," Cal said, feeling yet another uncontrollable wave of dislike for his uncle's wife. Was there ever a time her manner with people wasn't freezing? Oddly enough, he seemed to get the lion's share of her better moments. "Mina is a sweet, respectful, responsible girl. You should be grateful to her for the help."

"Grateful is the *last* thing I am," Janis huffed.

Somehow they got through lunch, with Janis throwing Amber malevolent looks across the table. Obviously she had moved up to the top of Janis's hit list. She had to keep telling herself that Janis had problems. But it seemed that at least some of her problems were by choice. Afterwards, Eliot took his wife by the elbow, moving her away with a polite, "Excuse us." It looked very much like Janis was digging in her heels, refusing to go. Women had been stran- gled for less.

Amber found herself asking Cal quietly if Janis had found him earlier on.

He eyed her with nagging worry. "I know this sounds weird, but I swear Janis could find me anywhere!"

To him it obviously presented a great mystery. Amber moved closer in, to whisper low, "And why is that, do you suppose?"

"How the hell should I know?"

Later Fitz offered a comment. "Poor lady! It's the PND then, is it?"

"I thought the condition was more civil than that." Cal was so mortified by Janis's behaviour that he skipped any excuses. He put his hand on the vet's shoulder, deliberately changing the subject. "By the way, I forgot to ask you, Is Charlie Morrissey recovering okay?"

Fitz shook his head. "No, he's still pretty crook."

"Crook in the head as well." Cal tapped his forehead. "That was a fool thing he did, trying to pick up a taipan by the tail."

Fitz gave a snort of laughter. "Drunk at the time. Drink always fuels stupidity." He turned to Amber, who was standing quietly. "I must say it's been a great treat to meet you, Amber. I don't need to tell you to watch that skin of yours in the sun."

Amber had to ask herself, why hadn't he?

"We'll look after her, Fitz," Cal assured him. "There's a ton of sun block on tap. I tell you that every time I see you."

"Too late, m'boy!"

"Wrong attitude, Fitzy," Cal pointed out, half turning his shoulder. "Ah, here's Eliot back again. You two can go off. I'll meet you a little later on. I want to fix Amber up with a horse to ride. She tells me she's good."

"Which means she is." Fitz gave Amber another warm, approving smile. This was a young lady who mightily impressed him. He had never known what to make of Eliot's second wife. The first one had been an angel, gone to God. This one might have strayed from the other place. Even before the little fellow had arrived no one could have called Janis MacFarlane pleasant. It wasn't a marriage that had been planned in heaven.

Almost immediately, Amber settled on her choice. She picked out a handsome coal-black gelding called Horatio, a seven-year-old ex-racehorse that had won handsomely for Cal's grandfather, Clive Erskine, only to be told that the gelding was too strong for her. Too mercurial by temperament.

"You haven't seen me ride yet," she said, affronted. The big gelding stood some seventeen hands high, but she was convinced she could ride him.

"We'll fix you up with something else." He ignored her tone. "What about this one now?" They moved down the line of stalls. "Star Belle. Isn't she beautiful? A bright chestnut almost the colour of your hair. Star Belle is another ex-race-horse. She's a little bit skittish with a new rider, but if you can handle her she'll settle down nicely."

"Sure you can trust me to have a go?" she challenged dryly, showing the mare her hand.

"I'd like nothing better than to trust you, Amber." He smiled, but the expression in his eyes was oceans deep.

"We've got issues, haven't we? They pop up all the time."

"It takes time to build back eroded confidence and trust."

"Loss of trust is a fact of life, Cal." She shrugged, still petting the responsive mare. "It's hard at first, but I don't think we really have an option but to reach out again. If we do everything in our power to avoid getting hurt, we'll never get to know what real love means."

"And you *really* loved him?" he mocked, when he was hurting with the desire to touch her. Pull her into his arms. Cover the beautiful creamy skin of her face with kisses, before settling ecstatically on her mouth—full, luscious, made to be kissed. If he had to describe his picture of the perfect woman it would be Amber Wyatt.

"I might ask, did you really love Brooke?" Amber countered, unnerved by the quality of his glance. It was like a mirror giving back her own desire. Stupid to allow a flash of jealousy for his ex-fiancée to mar it. But human enough, she supposed.

"I must have been in love with her at some stage. That's all you need to know."

"Ditto with Sean. I don't hate him. Maybe that's a telling thing. I despise him. That's entirely different. At any rate, his marriage to your cousin is no longer causing me grief."

"I'm glad to hear it." In fact it was a big relief. "But doesn't it prove you never really loved him?"

She gave him a defeated look. "I'm afraid you could be right. It's a little hard getting used to the idea I was such a rotten judge."

"Maybe we only have an *idea* of the people we love," he mused.

"Very likely. But what you see is what you get with me, MacFarlane. Now, why don't I show you how good a rider I am?"

He laughed. How could he not? She entertained him. "I'm telling you I can't wait. You look great in tight jodhpurs at any rate."

Despite herself she blushed. "They're not too tight, are they?" She didn't think she had put on weight.

"On the contrary, they're *perfect*! They need to be tight. If I were a better adjusted man I could really fancy you, Ms Wyatt."

"I think the fancying got out of hand at the wedding, don't you?"

"One of those instant inexplicable bondings," he suggested very dryly.

"Or a pretty powerful chemical reaction."

"Either way, it was great." He rested a hand lightly on her

silk-covered shoulder. Just a gesture but it sent a series of shock waves through her very receptive body. She couldn't recall a touch like it.

In the end, he made her parade round and round the exercise yard before he was satisfied, making her finish with a working gallop.

"You'll do!" Afterwards he lifted his arms so she had to slip down between him and the chestnut mare.

Her breasts were grazing his chest. She pulled back before she went to pieces. Behind her the mare whinnied. "I knew I would!" She tried for a cheeky smile, not easy when she was beset by desires she mightn't get the chance to fulfil.

He had to be feeling the same because he muttered, "I want to kiss you."

"Okay." She took a deep preparatory breath. The two of them were taking big risks, but the temptation was too powerful to resist.

His mouth came over hers as though he knew just what she wanted. At first it was soft and easy, a sort of learning experience, then she heard the groan in his throat before he pulled her in closer. The kiss deepened, changed character. His hand sought and found her breast, moving over it in an exquisite caress. Their lower bodies were pressed together, as if yearning to fuse as nature intended. This was what it meant to play with fire.

"Cal…" Her voice sounded unnaturally shaky. "This is so…"

"I know." He lifted his head, his hands dropping to her hips. "Just reaching out. Don't move. Not for a minute."

"I don't think I can." It was the solemn truth.

He continued to hold her. "Do you want this to come to anything, Amber?" He lifted her chin so he could stare into her eyes.

"I don't know what you're offering," she said. "I didn't see this coming."

"And you think I did?"

"So is it a good feeling or a scary feeling?"

For answer he bent his dark head and kissed her again. "Both. But let's say you make me feel more than I've ever felt before."

It was some admission coming from him.

Weeks sped by in a dazzle of excitement. Janis had been more or less forced into accepting the new regime that, thankfully, was getting encouraging results. Amber had taken to giving little Marcus a soothing massage after his nightly bath—something she had once seen demonstrated by a close friend, a mother of two, and to her delight he loved it. Marcus was getting much more sleep, as were his sleep-deprived parents. The entire household was hoping and praying that Janis's tensions would ease. But, if they did, she didn't show it. Truth be told, Janis seemed to get meaner, even if she was less vocal about it. That had to be a plus.

She did, however, do everything in her power to avoid Amber, who was getting a little tired of it. When it came right down to it, Amber had effected the changes. But no thanks there. Amber might have been a highly paid mother's helper. Disturbingly, she had the feeling that Janis hated her. Or maybe it wasn't her personally. Janis would hate any woman who took Cal MacFarlane's eye. Both Cal and his uncle appeared to be misreading the situation. Much as she wanted to give Janis the benefit of the doubt, Amber couldn't help thinking that Janis was simply hiding behind the label of PND and, in doing so, missing out on one of the greatest gifts in life—the bottomless well of love a mother had for her child.

Wasn't she then to be pitied? A miracle was in order here. But sadly miracles didn't occur all that often in life.

Janis badly needed a fresh start in her own home. Amber knew she would have wanted a home of her own. Eliot couldn't have it both ways. His wife and child were his top priorities. Back in the city, Janis might try a lot harder. There was plenty of help readily to hand. Surely she had made female friends over the years, even if she was estranged from her mother?

She wanted to toss up a few ideas with Cal, though she knew she was winging close to danger. She couldn't, for instance, try him out on, *Janis seems overly attached to you.* She would have to pack her bags, when she had never been happier in her life. Still, she made it her business to stop him one morning when he was almost out of the door. The man seemed to be getting up earlier and earlier and working later. He put in a full day's hard work and then some.

"Cal, could I have a word with you?" She hurried down the timber staircase.

He swung back, looking so damned glamorous she gulped. "If you make it quick," he clipped.

She tried to find her voice. He was the very picture of Action Man, a red bandana sweatband style around his head, raven locks curling over the top. The temperatures were climbing as they moved into high summer. The bandana would keep the sweat out of his eyes. It made him look so dashing, so unbelievably sexy, that she was hit by a dizzy spasm and had to rest against the balustrade. Little tremors were running up, down, all over her body. Day by day she was leaving all sense of caution behind. What else could she do? Cal MacFarlane was a revelation!

"Hey, are you okay?" Cal couldn't suppress the note of worry. This beautiful, never complaining woman, was his guest, yet she was handling everything like a highly paid employee. He was so much in her debt it was beginning to really bother him. Right from the beginning he had seen her in a number of stressful situations. She always acted in a manner he understood and approved. It was getting harder and harder to fault her. He had all but given up trying. What would he do if she vanished from his life? He wasn't playing any game. He was certain she wasn't playing a game, either. The truth was he wanted her to be *always* there, an integral part of his life. Damn it, the *centre* of his life. He was a man living with a secret.

What he hadn't thought could happen *had* happened.

Too late now, MacFarlane.

She continued on down the stairs, unaware of his thoughts, but hugging close that note of concern. "Sure,' she answered happily. She knew he and some of the men had already started to bring in the clean skins from the desert fringe in preparation for the big muster. She had heard with horror from Dee of the death of a station hand a few years back. The man had taken a fall from his spooked horse and was crushed to death. Since then Amber had been trying hard to block the image. Trying hard not to think of Cal in some life-threatening situation, even though she knew he confronted them on a daily basis. His well-being was vitally important to her.

"You'd tell me if you weren't?" Cal's brows knotted as he stared down at her.

Of a sudden she was feeling strong and ready, as though her energy had fed off his. "Don't worry, I'm not about to burn out."

"I *am* worried," he said. "I want you to get out more. Enjoy yourself. The plan wasn't to have you stuck in the house."

"Look, it's all happening. I have a really good feeling about Marcus. From now on he should start to thrive."

"You really like him, don't you?" He smiled, his beautiful eyes full of a mesmerizing glitter.

"Like him? I love him. He's a dear little fellow. He just had a rough start. Look, I won't hold you up now, Cal. You're obviously in a hurry."

"I'll give you ten minutes. How will that be?"

"Let's walk outside." She started to move to the door.

"Get your hat," he said in a no-nonsense voice.

"You got it, boss." She hurried away. When she returned she was wearing a wide-brimmed straw hat atop her hair and tied it at the nape with an inky-blue ribbon to match her tank top.

The need to *head things off at the pass*, so pressing at the beginning, had lost focus. No bigger risk than giving your heart away. He knew that. Even so, Cal surrendered to the magic of having Ms Wyatt around. He reached out a lazy hand and pulled the ribbon from her hair. As expected, it set her magnificent mane free, every conceivable shade of red, copper and gold. "A little bit of provocation, is it?" he asked, pocketing the ribbon, then flipping down the brim she had deliberately turned up all the way round to get his reaction.

"Who said you could pinch my ribbon?"

"Why, do you want it back?"

Oh, that glitter in his eyes! "Keep it. Put it under your pillow. Dream of me."

"What else can I do, since it seems too darned hard to get you into my bed?"

She looked up sharply, then smiled. "Haven't we agreed to get to know one another better, Cal? Sleeping with you could be as dangerous as jumping off a cliff."

"I'm game if you are."

The sensuality in his voice reeled her in. "Maybe I've got more to lose?" she suggested very seriously. "It can be worse for women."

"Nonsense!" His answer was blunt. "Okay, Amber. For you, I can wait. Maybe you'll start to want me as much as I want you."

She stood there with sensation nearly sweeping her off her feet. "Oh, I *want* you all right, but things are moving very fast, don't you agree?"

"Maybe they *have* to when our time is limited. What happens when they want you back? And they will."

"Don't talk about it," she begged. "I want to stay here for a long, long time."

"*I* won't be sending you away," he said. "Count on it. And don't dare turn that brim back again."

She laughed. "I've never had a man outside my dear father pay so much attention to protecting my skin."

He ran a finger down her cheek. "It's called meaning well. Your skin's great. Let's keep it that way." He was back to the bantering style he adopted when things got intense. Inside, Cal's nerves were stretched taut. "My mother used to wear big-brimmed straw hats like that," he said in a faintly melancholy voice. "She was beautiful, too."

"So when did you first decide you wanted nothing more to do with her?" Amber asked as gently as she could. There was a lot of unresolved feeling here. A mother was forever part of one's identity.

Instantly his body language radiated warning. "It's too long ago to remember."

"Is it?" She stared up at him, suddenly seeing him as a proud and handsome young boy.

"Don't *do* this, Amber," he warned, his green eyes aglitter.

She looked away across the garden, the air wavery in the heat. "Thought I'd give it a shot. Deep down I think you feel badly about the whole sorry situation. The trouble is, Cal, if you let your grievances go on too long, they become part of you like a second skin."

He took a minute to answer. "You know, you were wasted in television. You should have given psychoanalysis a shot."

"Hey, there's still time," she said, trying for breeziness. "All I'm saying is, where there's a will, there's a way. I'm like you. I mean well."

His firm mouth twitched. "Then could I remind you that a couple of wasted minutes have gone past. What's on your mind?"

She wasn't such a fool that she didn't know she had put a

serious dent in his armour. "We're friends, aren't we, Cal?" she asked, fixing her gaze on his brooding face. "You're happy we're friends? Friendship is important. Maybe more important than sex."

He laughed, beginning to unwind. "Hell, Amber, I liked you right off. Of course we're friends. It's not the *perfect* relationship. Don't knock sex, but I guess it will have to do."

"Want to tell me what the perfect relationship *is*?" she asked.

"I'd love to. I will. But it would take time. I don't have it at the moment. The men will be waiting on me for their orders. I think I can guess your question in one—When are you going to tell Eliot to take a break away with his wife?"

She nodded. "I'm not sure Jingala is the best place for them long-term. Janis might be a whole lot happier if she had a home of her own."

"Gets my vote," he answered tautly. "It's Janis who won't move away."

"But she told me otherwise." She stared at him, puzzled. "She understood they were to live in Melbourne but Eliot brought her here."

The severity was back. "So when did you have this little chat?"

"Hey, listen, don't get cranky with me." She placed a calming hand on his arm.

He stared down at the sight of her creamy skin, a stark contrast to his dark tan. "Amber, the last thing I'd do is vent my wrath on you. You're a godsend. This has turned into a dilemma in more ways than one. I'd like to put as much distance as I can between Janis and myself, but then I lose the uncle I've lived with all my life and love. Plus the fact I also lose out on seeing Marcus grow up."

"Well, I understand that," she said with characteristic empathy. "But you'll have children of your own. Eliot and family would always be welcome. Who knows, they might add to it."

"For God's sake!" He reacted with extreme impatience. "I couldn't tell you how many times I've heard Jan yelling she hated being pregnant. She swore she'd never allow herself to get pregnant again. I, for one, believe her. And you're wrong. I don't care what Jan told you. It was *Jan* who convinced Eliot she wanted to come out to Jingala. You've had time to get to know Eliot. You must see he would have done whatever she asked. They were to live in Melbourne, but at some point Jan had a change of heart."

She fell in love. A huge mistake on every count.

The wrong kind of love could be a sickness.

"Jan's spirits might lift if you convinced Eliot to take her away for a holiday," she bravely soldiered on.

"And I haven't tried? What the hell keeps her here?" he asked. "She has never shown the slightest interest in the station and station life. She's not in the least like you. She sees no beauty—gets no pleasure—from her environment. She doesn't ride and she doesn't intend to learn. Horses are another one of her hates. So what's the attraction?"

To her absolute horror, Amber muttered a thoughtful, "Um…"

"You have an answer?' He fired up.

He really was a high-voltage man. "I do, but I'm not sure I should go with it."

"Now's as good a time as any," he told her with a darkening frown. "Spit it out, Amber."

"You can't guess?"

He retorted by putting his hand beneath her chin. Just the barest hint of force. "I'd like you to tell me. You're the oracle around here."

"And you don't like it?' Just looking up at him made her heart pound.

"On the contrary, I'm obliged to you." He relented with a smile.

"That's a relief! But I'm beginning to think telling you might be more than my life's worth."

"Can you prove what you think?" The challenge was back.

"Not one hundred and ten per cent, no."

"Then I'll take a pass on it until you can. For now, I'm off. Don't think I'm not grateful to you for all you've done, Amber. When I have the time I'm going to buy you the biggest present you've ever seen. I will speak to Eliot again. I'll do it tonight."

"Insist!" Amber transmitted her own seriousness. "Your uncle will take notice."

CHAPTER NINE

MID-MORNING a very unexpected thing happened. Brooke Rowlands arrived on Jingala, piloting her own Cessa 310.

How cool was that!

Was it a chance occurrence? Or had she come on a specific mission? Had she despaired of getting an invitation and taken matters into her own hands? One might well wonder. All except Janis. Janis, unbeknown to anyone, had sent Brooke an email telling her, in effect, if she still wanted to land her man she had better get over to Jingala chop-chop.

Even Janis herself didn't know why she'd done it. She was ill with her own tortured feelings for Cal. Horrified that such a thing had happened to her. She had thought she had her life under control. She had been reasonably content. She never expected to be happy. Happiness was for simpler souls. She regarded herself as a highly intelligent, complex woman, wound tight, much like the heroines of fiction. She had met and married a distinguished man. Rich, of course. She wouldn't have looked sideways at anyone with less than fifty million dollars. Hardly worth the effort. But the MacFarlane family wealth combined came in at over a billion. She had checked it out. The old man, Cal's grandfather Clive Erskine, had at least six billion, not that she had any chance of getting her hands on that. The MacFarlanes had a fine family name.

Another big plus. They were one of the biggest landowners in the country, with a massive four million hectares spread over a dozen properties right across the State of Queensland. So marriage had come at a time when she'd doubted she would give herself to anyone at all. After all, she had the brains to make her own way in life.

Never for a moment had she anticipated what would happen to her. It had come like a lightning bolt, flattening her in the process. A monumental strike!

She didn't love her husband. Love hadn't come into it. It had seemed like a great career move at the time. She wanted to be pampered. She wanted to be rich. She wanted to establish herself in society. It wasn't as though she could actually say that she had ever loved anyone. She had thought herself incapable of it and wasn't by any means desperate about it. Some people were natural born loners.

Until she'd laid eyes on Cal MacFarlane.

Cal, her husband's nephew, with his enormous charisma and those glittering green eyes!

It was lunacy. But for a while it was glorious! To *feel* as she did! It was so extravagant, so real that she didn't have a single moment of remorse, or shame, much less guilt. She was always on the verge of telling him. Later she would spend endless time thanking God she hadn't. The humiliation would have crushed her. But back then! Finally, at the age of thirty-four, she had fallen in love. She was human after all. She would never think of herself as a loner ever again. Only it was her cruel fate to learn the hard way that it was all a terrible mistake—a mistake made all the more bitter because, from the very day of her wedding, Cal had kept his distance. Restraint she had expected, the situation being what it was. But the searing truth, impossible at first to grasp, was that he didn't *like* her, much less desire her. She had divined that once the haze had started to clear. It had come as a tremendous shock.

How could such a thing happen? She had thought the powerful attraction just *had* to be mutual. But Cal gave her a wide berth. He loved his uncle. They had a great relationship, when she had never had a significant relationship in her life. Her top businesswoman mother, by and large, had ignored her most of the time she was growing up. Having a child didn't sit comfortably with her career-oriented mother. These days, burdened with her own extremely difficult, demanding child, she had more empathy for her mother. Having Marcus didn't sit comfortably with her, either. Neither woman was the nurturing kind. So mother and daughter shared a trait. Where was this mystical, magical bond she was supposed to experience with her child? Maybe she might have felt it had she and *Cal* created Marcus together. But Cal had no sexual interest in her. She could taste the steely humiliation in her mouth.

It was that interfering, sickeningly capable fire-head, Amber Wyatt, who had somehow established a strong connection with Marcus, who had definitely taken Cal's fancy. So desperately in love with him herself—how did one go about killing love?—she could easily read the signs. It disturbed her terribly that Amber Wyatt might succeed where she had failed. By necessity, she had to let Ms Wyatt organise the baby's needs, but no way was she going to stand by and allow such a woman to convince Cal she was just the kind of woman—the kind of *wife*—he needed. For some reason she didn't fully understand, she didn't feel threatened by the idea of Brooke Rowlands coming back into Cal's life. If Brooke could hang in there and Cal eventually married her she would know his heart wasn't in it. It would be an arrangement like hers with Eliot.

She could live with that.

Amber was on her way back from the stables after her routine morning ride when Dee appeared on the pathway. She had her arms extended frantically, as if trying to block a runaway horse.

"Everything okay?" Instantly Amber was beset by panic. When she had left the house Marcus was perfectly fine. Had something happened?

"The baby's fine," Dee cried, knowing how important little Marcus's well-being had become to Amber. "It's somethin' else. Did ya happen to notice a plane comin' in?"

"Sure." She hadn't taken a lot of notice. Even during her short stay, light aircraft had been flying in and out of the station. Freight, supplies, the vet et cetera.

Dee reached her, grasping her arm. "Listen, love," she panted, "you'll have to go back and warn Cal. He won't be at all happy about this.'

"About what, Dee?" Amber was confused.

"About Brooke showin' up." Dee looked less than delighted. "She's on her way up to the house."

That earned Amber's full attention. Cal's ex-fiancée had come calling? The woman he had most certainly slept with. It was highly unlikely they hadn't consummated their relationship. "What does she want?" She could hear the anxious note in her voice, but Dee didn't appear to notice.

"Why, to try again, girl," she said, heaving a deep breath. "She'll *never* give up, on the principle that Cal won't be able to hold out. 'Course she always comes with an excuse. An invitation to some 'do' or other. Some books or CDs she thinks the family might like. Random check on Janis and the baby. Any excuse will do. We can't talk now. You'll have to find Cal. He's at the Four Mile. Well, get goin', love!" Dee urged Amber on with a stout tap on the shoulder.

This time she took a fresh horse, the handsome coal-black gelding, Horatio, her first choice. Cal had convinced her to get her bearings first, as well as ride her way back into form before she took on the big gelding. Today she was ready. The morning's ride, always in the company of winged formations of birds, had been delightful. Star Belle was the smoothest mover. Now that she had got used to Amber up on her back they made a fine pair, horse and rider. She had promised Cal she would stick to a certain radius and, mindful of possible dangers, she had obeyed him implicitly. Eagerly she waited for the time when he would join her for a long ride. He had promised her he would, but she knew how things were revving up on the station.

Up on Horatio's back, she felt a tiny twinge of nerves. This was another animal altogether, much bigger, with longer, stronger legs. She bent low over the gelding's ebony neck, keeping her voice down to a calm, low pitch to reassure the animal of her presence. "All's well, boy. All's well. Just do your best for me."

Out in the grasslands without mishap, she soon discovered this was a horse that was all fluid power. No wonder Horatio had dazzled in his heyday. Obviously the horse was demonstrating his willingness to trust her. She felt over time they could build up quite a rapport. If she kept heading north-west, following the line of coolibah over-hung billabongs, she would come on the Four Mile where the cows and calves were being herded. It was even possible she might be invited to join in damper and billy tea. She had met most of the men by now. Most of them were very shy around women, which didn't stop them ogling Amber, but very discreetly. What was she going to say to Cal? *Boy, are you in trouble or not! Your girlfriend's here.*

What if he answered, *Great!*

This had been a time of intense excitement but also great uncertainty for her. A testing time. She thought of it as going on a journey. She thought Cal was going along with her. Could she be proved wrong? She'd have to make a point of asking Dee just how often in recent times Brooke Rowlands had come calling. Although Janis had made it her business to tell her that Cal and Brooke had slept together on her last stay, she wasn't at all persuaded. Maybe she couldn't *bear* to be persuaded. There was a good deal more to learn about Cal. He was one complex man and his mistrust of women was in-grained. His mother leaving at a critical stage of his develop-ment had kick-started that condition. His fiancée betraying him with, of all people, a friend had entrenched it. Women weren't to be trusted. Or forgiven. Men weren't to be trusted either. Not a woman alive would dispute that.

Amber reviewed the developing situation with some trepi-dation. Brooke could still pose a threat. Life could be aston-ishingly uncertain. Cal had become engaged hoping for happiness, after all. But no one could take happiness as an absolute certainty. There were always risks. Always unan-swered questions. Maybe Brooke's visit would clear up all those vital points?

Approaching the Four Mile she reined the big gelding in. "We've made it, my friend!" There was elation in that.

She rode quietly into camp. There was a whole lot of ribaldry passing to and fro among the stockmen but, when they sighted her, silence fell like a blanket.

"The boss here?" she called to the seemingly stunned group. She might well have been an apparition.

Instantly there was rectitude. The head stockman was the first to respond. He touched a respectful hand to his battered hat. "Go get him, miss." He strode off in one direction, but Cal confounded them all by appearing from another, cool eyes flashing.

"Say it isn't so!" He indicated for her to take her feet out of the stirrups before sweeping her out of the saddle. "That's not Horatio?"

They were standing so close. His arm had slid around her waist, bringing their hips together. His polished skin gleamed gold with sweat. She could feel beads of moisture start trick-ling between her breasts. Their relationship was more than ripe for sex. But, once they took that step, both of them would be altering their worlds. Fate had led her on this fantastic journey. In the process it had showed her her true nature. She was a passionate woman—passionately in love. It had never been remotely like this with Sean. Sean's betrayal had actually done her an enormous favour. It had opened a new door on life. A life she was rapidly coming to hope was full of promise.

"Horatio it is!" She spoke breezily when her blood was sizzling. "I thought I'd give it a shot. Actually, we went very well together."

"You know what they say? Pride comes before a fall." He looked back over his shoulder. "Take Horatio, would you, Toby."

"Sure, boss." Toby came on the double to collect the gelding.

Cal led her into the shade. "Did you expect me to be im-pressed?" There wasn't the most approving note in his voice.

"No need to get testy." She glanced up at his handsome high-cheekboned face, shadowed by the brim of his hat. His light eyes were such a shock. "I took my usual ride on Star Belle in ac-cordance with your wishes, Mr MacFarlane, but returning to the house I met up with Dee with a message to pass on. I needed a fresh horse, okay? No worries, anyway. Horatio and I are pals."

"You could have had trouble controlling him," he said, wanting to grab hold of her and keep her safe. "Horatio doesn't take to everybody." That was the sorry truth.

"Is that so? Well, I have to tell you it was love at first sight. Ever happen to you?" She stared challengingly into his cool green eyes.

"It has, up until recently, been a point of pride with me to keep a level head, Ms Wyatt. But, if such a thing happens, you'll be the first to know."

"Can I count on it?" There was a betraying wobble in her voice.

"I've said so, haven't I?"

"Right." She dipped her head before her rioting feelings became too obvious. "Do you want to hear the message or not?"

He gave a laugh, half maddened, half amused. "Amber, that was the Rowlands Cessna that flew in. Do you really think I don't know what's happening over my own land? Who is it— Peter and Brooke, or Brooke on her own?"

She mustered a smile. "I'm delighted to tell you it's Brooke on her own. It's a wonder you didn't *feel* it." She lightly tapped her breast. "You know, here in the heart."

"That's it, fire away." He brought up his hand, passing it over his eyes. "Could you do yet another thing for me? Go back to the homestead and tell Brooke I'll be away for a few days."

"You speak in jest, sir?" His face was so perfectly straight.

"Hell, I half mean it," he groaned.

"So where would you be if you decided to chicken out?"

"Fair question." He reached out and yanked her thick copper plait.

"Gone bush?" she suggested. "I suppose, if you wanted, you'd have a chance of pulling that off. Unless you really want to see her. Do you?" She spoke lightly but her expression was alert.

"You're kidding. I'm *dying* to see her."

Her heart lunged. "I thought you'd moved on?"

"Me?" He leaned in very close. "For such a beautiful, intelligent, perceptive woman you're mighty unsure of yourself."

"Put it another way. My emotions are fragile. So just don't go treading on them."

"As if I would!" He stared into her eyes. "We've got to trust one another, Amber. Or learn how." He broke into a quotation, his voice deepening with some emotion that caused a delicious shiver to run down her back. " 'I have spread my dreams under your feet. Tread softly because you tread on my dreams.'" That said, he reverted to his normal crisp tone. "Isn't that a poem?"

"Yeats. At least I think it's Yeats. You have a great voice, Cal. It's a bit like Russell Crowe's. Or even Mel Gibson's. Anyway, I've delivered my message. Now it's up to you. And to think I rode all this way for nothing. You already knew."

He laughed quietly. "Would a cup of billy tea make it up to you?"

"I thought you'd never ask."

Brooke Rowlands couldn't have been nicer. A young woman of style. Well, she had to have something for the Cattle Baron to have fallen in love with her in the first place, Amber reasoned. She wasn't proud of the fact that she felt more than a few flashes of some unwelcome emotion that had to be jealousy. She wasn't a jealous woman by nature. She had never felt jealous of Georgie Erskine, which was odd. But she found she really cared about Cal and Brooke's relationship. Was it firmly in the past or not? It would be too, too *awful* if Cal were to decide somewhere along the line he wanted Brooke, the countrywoman, back. Confounding things happened every day of the week. Human behaviour was beyond rational explanation.

On Jingala Amber was showing remarkable resilience. She never gave Sean a thought now. He was history. She wasn't sure what that said about her. All she knew was that meeting Cal MacFarlane had proved a life-altering experience. It had nothing whatever to do with warding off the pain and humiliation of her broken engagement. Something absolutely unique had happened. She was certain enough of own powers of attraction, backed up by Cal's words and actions, to recognize that Cal had been plunged into a similar situation. But he wasn't a *trusting* guy. The thing was, attraction took on its own dimensions. What *she* felt was *powerful*. Brooke, who had been desirable enough to land Cal in the first place, obviously wanted a second chance. Who could blame her?

What exactly did Cal, the object of all their longings, feel? With the arrival of Brooke on the scene, Amber came to the full realisation that she wanted him all to herself. The world could offer her no more than Cal MacFarlane.

As soon as she strode through the front door, a strikingly attractive brunette with a glossy chin-length bob, a deep fringe to show off her lovely big brown eyes, a great figure in designer jeans and a red tank top that tightly hugged her pert breasts surged from the Great Room.

"Amber Wyatt! I may call you Amber? You're even more beautiful in person than you are on our TV screens. I'm one of your fans." Appearing slightly breathless, the young woman held out her hand. Amber took it, feeling silky, pampered skin. There was something underlying the cordial manner but Amber put it down to understandable concern. Women could spot possible rivals in a nanosecond.

"It's Brooke, isn't it?" Amber smiled back. It was hard not to. Brooke sounded so sincere, earnest even. She had to be aware that during her stint in front of the cameras she had won over a lot of viewers.

"Of course it's Brooke," Janis's voice rang out from behind them. "Where's Cal?"

"Patience, patience. I only saw him briefly. He's right in the thick of it."

"I bet you went looking for him," Janis countered.

Brooke Rowlands pre-empted any retort by linking her arm through Amber's and turning her towards the Great Room. "You'd like coffee?"

"Love some," Amber said. "First I'd like to freshen up after my morning ride."

"You enjoy riding?"

Why the note of surprise? "Sure do."

"So what horse did Cal let you take?"

You'd swear it was a test. "Belle Star is my usual mount. She's lovely. Very sweet-tempered when you get to know her. I have taken Horatio out. A different horse altogether."

"Then you must ride very well." Brooke didn't sound all that pleased to hear it.

"My dad put me on my first pony at age six," Amber explained. "I love horses."

"Dreadful, unpredictable animals!" Janis shuddered as though life was hard enough without having to contend with horses.

Amber and Brooke, both fine horsewomen, ignored her. "Give me ten minutes," Amber begged, turning towards the staircase.

"How did you know Brooke was here?" Janis called after her, like some detective.

Amber's heart skipped a beat but she turned back casually. "Just as Brooke knows my face, I know hers. You're often in the society pages, aren't you, Brooke?" For one awful moment she thought Brooke was going to deny it. She hadn't, in fact, ever laid eyes on Brooke Rowlands before. There were certainly no silver-framed photographs of her in Cal's study.

But Brooke gave a gratified smile. "I do love to get away to the city from time to time. You can't imagine how relieved I am the paparazzi don't follow me around."

As promised, Amber was downstairs ten minutes later, having dashed under the shower and re-dressed in a short loose kaftan that wafted around her body. First she checked in with Dee in the kitchen.

"Find the boss?" Dee asked in a conspiratorial whisper, though no one could have heard her even if they were hiding behind the door.

"My horse could have found Cal on his own." Amber smiled. "He said he'll be out of town for a few days."

"I bet he'd like to be!" Dee muttered, never having forgiven Brooke for betraying Cal.

"I thought he might like having her around?" Amber ventured uncertainly.

Dee gave a grunt. "Been chattin' to Mrs MacFarlane?"

"Anyway, how's our little sweetheart?" Amber broke off a couple of seedless white grapes, popping them in her mouth.

"He's fast asleep." Dee gave a satisfied smile. "I've set Mina to watching over the dear little soul. I tell you, Marcus is a totally different baby. All your doin', my girl!"

"Modesty prevents me from taking the credit, Dee." Amber smiled.

"Don't interrupt me. We're all indebted to you." Dee spoke with feeling. "And you can count Mrs MacFarlane in, though she'd die before she'd ever admit it."

"Let's give her a chance, Dee." Amber gently touched Dee's shoulder. "I don't like to be *too* judgemental."

"Me, either." Dee sighed. "At the same time, I can't condone her behaviour. Best go back to them, love. Brooke will be acting like you're her new best friend, but be on your guard. She's pleasant enough, I'll grant ya that. She might have thought she could get away with playin' around, but Cal will never forgive her or have her back.'

"Surely she can gauge that?" Amber asked. Could it be true that Brooke had recently received a measure of encouragement? "What about when she stayed before? Janis was insistent they were still…*close*."

Dee snorted. "Cal would have put bars on his doors and windows if he could. There was no hanky-panky, love. Set your mind at rest. No sneaking up and down the corridors. Now, I'll have coffee and some nice little cup cakes ready in a few minutes. Someone has to spare Brooke Mrs

MacFarlane's endless railing against life. If you ask me, she acts more like a woman in the throes of a mad passion than a new mother with a medical problem."

Amber had already formed that opinion but it still gave her a shock to hear it more or less confirmed by Dee—someone more in a position to know.

They all came together again at dinner. Brooke had ridden out that afternoon in search of Cal, coming back to the homestead an hour later to lament, "I couldn't find him anywhere." Amber didn't feel able to offer a comment. Cal must have led the muster into the depths of the lignum swamps before making his return to the homestead alone.

Brooke regrouped with seduction clearly on her mind. She looked lovely in a short silk dress in a gorgeous shade of blue. Her make-up was impeccable and her glossy fringe drew attention to her big brown eyes.

Amber, for all her qualms, enjoyed looking at her. The Cattle Baron would hardly be human if he didn't appreciate what a sight for sore eyes she was. Brooke Rowlands was a glamour girl and very flirtatious by nature. She was certainly giving Cal the treatment, by no means throwing in the towel.

And she was a lot of fun. A most welcome change from Janis, who sat looking exhausted, pushing the delicious food around her plate as though it deserved to be thrown out. Not that Brooke left Janis out of the conversation. She constantly made efforts to draw Janis in but she wasn't terribly successful if monosyllabic replies were anything to go on.

"Janis and I are planning a short trip away," Eliot, looking a good deal happier, at one point announced.

"Excuse me?" Janis turned on him so sharply that Amber winced.

Eliot didn't back down. "You need the break, my dear," he said with just the right amount of command. "We both do. Our darling boy has given you a hard time—not his fault, of course—but miraculously he appears to have settled."

"No miracle," Cal drawled, ~~savouring another~~ mouthful of a very fine Shiraz. "I'm sure Jan is happy to give Amber credit for bringing about a few changes."

"Amber, of course." Eliot saluted Amber with his wine-glass. He had thanked Amber over and over privately but he knew that thanking her on an occasion like this was like waving a red flag in front of his wife's nose.

"Well, that's grand then, isn't it?" Brooke exclaimed. "You'll be staying on to look after little Marcus, Amber?"

"Amber isn't a minder, Brooke," Cal broke in. "She's a miracle worker. Eliot and Jan can go away, happy in the knowledge that we're *all* here to look after Marcus."

"Excuse me, but I don't think I *want* to go away!" Janis threw up a hand, thus sending her wineglass—mercifully empty—over.

"Doctor's orders." Eliot attended swiftly to the wineglass.

"You're raving!" Janis drew back in her chair. "I haven't seen a doctor for ages. I don't need a doctor. I don't like doctors."

"You want to look after your own baby, is that it, Jan?" Brooke intervened with real kindness. She had tried to like Eliot's second wife but Janis MacFarlane was incredibly difficult to like. However had Eliot married her? Sex couldn't be the answer. Janis looked as if she'd scream the place down if ever a man came near her. Yet she had produced a child, as difficult a little soul as his mother from all accounts.

"My figure's gone." Janis made a very revealing answer. "I don't know my own body any more."

"It will come right again," Brooke assured her in a soothing tone. "You're way too thin. A short break seems just the thing, wouldn't you say?" She looked to the others to back her up.

"I have mentioned the Great Barrier Reef," Eliot said. "Sun and surf."

"What, with all the concern about skin cancer?" Janis's brows shot up. "You're raving! The sun will *kill* you, so you'd better watch out, Ms Wyatt."

"Ms Wyatt?" Brooke pulled a droll face, catching Amber's eye.

"I hate this trend of calling people by their first names right off," Janis explained loftily.

Cal gave a sardonic laugh. "Just as well you didn't go into public relations, Jan. You'd have had no future whatever."

Over coffee, Brooke asked if Amber would like to visit the Rowlands' station, Goorack. Brooke was Outback born and bred, which made her a hospitable young woman.

"I'd love to!" Amber replied with genuine warmth. She liked Brooke, for all her fall from grace. Most people would. Brooke was bright and friendly. She didn't blame her at all for trying to get Cal back. She understood it completely. She even understood Janis's sad fixation and her refusal to go away with her husband for a short break. How the marriage was going to work out, Amber didn't know. Divorce looked like the best option at this point, except—and a *huge* except— they shared a lasting bond. They had a small child desperately in need of tender loving care, not from well-meaning people around him, but from his mother.

Amber prayed that would happen. And happen soon. Janis MacFarlane might have a passion, but sadly it wasn't for motherhood.

Amber had been lying sleepless for about an hour, staring up at a moonlit ceiling. The ceiling stared back, offering no answers. She realized she had been straining to hear a baby's cry. Janis had been in such an odd mood, even for an odd woman. Eliot would have a job on his hands getting her to go away. Seeing Cal on a daily basis was something Janis clearly had to have. No future in that!

She was giving her pillows a hearty punch when an unmistakable summons came on her door. Hadn't she been half expecting it? Janis MacFarlane was too much under a hypnotic spell to go quietly. She threw on her robe, padding to the door.

Cal stood there, his arms holding on to the door frame, wide shoulders hunched.

"Another raid?" She tried for a joke, seeing the strain in his face. "Janis again?" She didn't want to go to Janis. She wanted to pull Cal inside. Sweep every scrap of caution under the Persian rug. Her body was aching for him. She was even ready to rope him in. Deep down she was sorry for Brooke. But she had to remind herself: all's fair in love and war.

"'Fraid so," he said, sounding as sexually deprived as she felt.

"Just when I was getting my hopes up," she felt emboldened to say, a splash of colour in her cheeks.

"I didn't say I won't be back."

"I didn't say I won't let you in."

"That's good. You're so darn beautiful I can't keep it a secret. I want to kiss every inch, every fold, every crevice of your sweet creamy body. That's for starters. Then I want to work around it with my tongue. I want to do *everything* you want." He broke off with a huge sigh. "Hell, I can't take this!"

"You mean we have to put the ravishing on hold." Statement not a question.

"I couldn't be unhappier about it, but the idea of a holiday has really got Janis going. You'd think she'd been sentenced to a stint in jail. You have to come. Eliot and I are stalled. She was trying to shake Marcus quiet."

Amber was stunned. This was a warning sign, impossible to ignore. "She didn't. She *couldn't*."

Cal ran a frustrated hand through his hair. "No one could call her a gentle soul. Not even with her own child. Are you coming?"

"Of course I'm coming. You didn't wake Brooke? You did consider her at one time for mother of your children."

"And I guess she'd make a good mother," he answered tersely. "Just not for *my* children."

"Maybe you'd better make sure she knows that. She's still in love with you."

"God forbid she should *stay* that way."

He sounded absolutely on the level. It should have allayed her fears, yet she said with a touch of disapproval, "Oh, you're cruel!"

"Tell me something I don't know." He grasped her arm, lucid green eyes sharpening over her body. "Isn't that a new robe?"

"You're paying me so many after hours visits I thought I'd better shake a new one out. It's a genuine Japanese silk kimono. Bought it on a trip to see the cherry blossoms. They don't come cheap. Not this quality. Glad you noticed."

"I've got used to noticing everything about you, Amber. Janis's behaviour would chill out the hottest-blooded male, but that's not happening here. What's *wrong* with the blessed woman? She's so utterly dissatisfied with her life—it's a total mess."

He'd hit it on the head. "Eliot has to assert himself. They need that break. Get life back into perspective. Janis is a married woman with a child. It's called responsibility. Commitment."

"If you ask me, she wants to put as much distance between herself and Eliot and the baby as she can." Cal spoke with a world of regret.

Brooke asked over breakfast, "Did I hear a lot of noise last night, or was I dreaming? I have to say I had one glass of wine too many."

"Just the baby," Amber explained the incident away. No matter how much she had wanted Cal to join her, little Marcus had got the vote.

"What the heck is wrong with Janis?" Brooke asked, lightly buttering a piece of toast. "A friend of mine suffered post-natal depression after her second baby. She was quite okay with the first. She said it was pretty bad but she got lots of love and support. From the very first time I met Janis… maybe I shouldn't say this—" she swept on "—Janis struck me as overwound. You know, the neurotic sort, with the main focus on themselves, what *they* need and want out of life. I guess having a baby might have worsened the condition. I can see how worried everyone is. Can I hold the little fellow before I go? I need to be back home by mid-afternoon."

"Of course you can!" Amber agreed straight away, pleased that Brooke had asked.

"I know this seems absolutely crazy—" Brooke was back to muttering behind her hand "—but Janis seems to have the hots for Cal. Tell me it isn't so?" She pinned Amber with her big brown eyes.

"Janis is fragile at the moment," Amber offered quietly. She didn't mention the huge fight that had broken out after Eliot and Janis had retired, an argument initiated by Janis and her aversion to leaving the homestead. Marcus had settled into his routine of sleeping quietly, only to be woken by his mother's high-pitched rant. It had been more than enough to set him off. It had taken Amber ages to quieten him after taking him down to her room.

"So have *you* got the hots for him?" Brooke asked. "Don't be offended. I have to ask. You're so beautiful…but I've never stopped loving him."

"Brooke, I don't know what's in Cal's mind." She hoped Brooke wouldn't press her further.

"So how long *have* you known him?" Brooke asked, intent on finding out.

"Only a matter of weeks."

"Long enough." Brooke fetched up a huge sigh. "He's terrific, isn't he?"

Amber poured them both a fresh cup of coffee. "Sure is," she said.

Cal returned to the house to see Brooke off. He had long since made the decision not to forgive her but it appeared he was undergoing some sort of sea change of late. And he knew since when. Since the arrival of Amber Wyatt into his life. She was making him over. Maybe making him a better man. He wouldn't be in the least surprised if she talked him into seeing his mother again. The perennial globetrotter, his mother spent some time in her own country. Would he ever forgive her? Could Amber persuade him to? He could only wait and see.

Brooke was trying hard for composure, but in the end she pulled Cal's head down to her. "I'm so sorry we didn't make it, Cal." Real tears stood in her eyes. "I'll always love you." She stood on tiptoe, pressing her mouth against his so passionately she would have left him in no doubt.

Amber, about to make her entrance to say her goodbyes and tee up a visit to Goorack, diplomatically stepped back a few paces, sheltering behind a luxuriant golden cane. She could hear the distressed note in Brooke's voice as though she had somehow divined that any further attempt to get him back would fail. Amber of the tender heart felt like offering condolences. At the same time she had to ask herself—if Cal and Brooke had still been engaged would he have asked her to Jingala?

The answer had to be a resounding *no*! So, at the end of the day, Brooke's loss was her gain. That was if she knew how to convince Cal of the depth and steadiness of her feelings. He in turn had to do the same thing for her. No greater risk than giving one's heart away. No spontaneous recovery. Healing took time.

To Brooke's great credit, her manner with Amber remained warm and friendly, so much so that Amber went along for the ride while Cal drove Brooke to Jingala's giant hangar where her Cessna was parked.

"It must be wonderful to be able to fly," Amber said dreamily as the Cessa lifted off the runway and climbed into the wild blue yonder.

"I'll teach you." Though his answer was abrupt, his hand was resting on her shoulder, his thumb absentmindedly caressing the bone.

"You think we will have that amount of time together?" She tipped her head so it lay along his hand.

"That's up to you, Amber." His caressing hand moved to her cheek. "I know this has had the elation of an adventure for you. I know you genuinely love the Outback. You see its wild beauty. Feel its mystique. But what of your career? You might suddenly go off and never return. Jingala will be something to look back on. God, you're beautiful enough to get into movies."

"There's a price to be paid for all that fame," she pointed out. "There's even a price to be paid for being on national television. I haven't told you about a few stalkers who caused me some grief. There is always some nutcase out there. Anyway, I've never had the slightest ambition to become a movie star, even supposing I got a break." She didn't mention that she had been approached some time back by a top agent for a lead part in a new television series. She had turned the role down.

"Okay." His handsome features were taut. "But loneliness is very threatening and it's a lonely life out here. The absence of so many things you're used to. I'll go further and say you don't really know what you'd be getting yourself into."

"So you *are* taking me seriously?" Her heart lifted in hope.

"You know damned well I'm taking you seriously." Intensity blazed out of his eyes. To prove it, he lowered his head to catch her mouth, kissing her so deeply that she found herself clutching him for support. "I want *you* in my bed," he groaned. 'No one else but you."

"But you fear I'll put a dent in your heart, then go away?" She pulled back a little so she could look into his eyes.

"Maybe that fear is chronic." He gave a harsh laugh. "I couldn't bear to have you, then lose you. Surely you can understand that?"

"It works both ways, Cal," she told him gently. "You have me, then you drive me away with your fears. I think you always carry the image of your mother in your mind, a beautiful woman who was unfaithful to her husband. Probably driven into an affair through sheer boredom or loneliness. Please don't cast me in that role."

"Did I say I have?" he asked with a note of anguish. "You've never known the pain of loneliness and isolation, Amber. *Have* you?"

"I think you're just trying to find reasons to reject me."

A faraway look came into his beautiful green eyes. "Hard to reject you when I'm hooked."

Elation filled every nerve, every fibre of her body. "You'd give up your freedom?"

"Would you?" He held her gaze.

"Gracious me, yes. Total commitment is a very serious business. That's why we're in this holding pattern. The other problem isn't going away."

"You mean Janis?" he asked impatiently. "What are we going to do about Janis? God, it ought to be the title for a psychological thriller. Except it's not funny. Eliot can't cope. He and Caro were so much in harmony, he doesn't know what's struck him with Jan. I know some people might deem his lack of action as gutless but he's far from that. I've seen him being incredibly brave. It's just he's a fish out of water in this situation, even if he *has* done his best. Jan has resisted all offers of help. So what next?"

"You ask, so I'll say. Eliot has to act. He's not *engaging* as much as he should."

"I know." Cal shook his dark head. "My fear is Janis wants to abandon Marcus."

"Mothers don't abandon their babies." The thought shocked her.

"Of course they do," he answered bluntly. "And this one *will*."

"She can't remain at Jingala."

"Why is it I feel you're trying to tell me something?" he asked sharply.

Amber looked away to where a flock of corellas had covered the branches of a river gum like fantastic white blossom. "It's not pretty," she warned.

He gritted his fine teeth. "For God's sake, Amber, let's hear it."

"Okay. You asked." She drew in a quivering breath. "Janis is in love with you."

His darkly tanned face visibly lost colour. "No, no, no, *no!*'

The tension was so palpable she could feel it on her skin. "I'm sorry, Cal, but I say it as I see it. Janis is infatuated with you. That's the reason she's so unhappy. It's not PND. The Flying Doctor people were right. It's not a mood disorder, something mood enhancers and good counselling can counteract. Her feelings are all tied up with *you*. You had your own experience with Brooke. I had mine with Sean. We can't love to order."

"Bloody hell, *no!*' he repeated, looking supremely outraged.

"Think about it."

"This is wrong!" He spoke roughly, green eyes flashing. "She's my uncle's wife. She's the mother of his child. I don't even *like* the woman and God knows I've tried. How could she be so disloyal?"

Amber gave him the only answer she knew. "It happens, Cal. Brooke still loves you. I suppose she'll regret her indiscretion to her dying day."

"Indiscretion! What a lightweight label. I didn't know about Janis." He looked and sounded extraordinarily tense.

"I know you didn't."

"Does Eliot know?"

"He may not have grasped the *depth* of her feelings," Amber said. "Doomed love can be awful. Both of us got a taste of that."

"Because we weren't really in love in the first place," he decided tautly. "They were *there*. That's all there is to it. Seeing Brooke beside you confirmed that for me."

At his admission her heart gave a great leap of joy, but she didn't follow up that revealing piece of information when his energy was focused on something else entirely.

"If what you say is even halfway true, I can see no happiness ahead for my uncle." Cal gave vent to a bitter sigh. "The situation is far more worrying for Marcus."

She shared his distress. "First step is to get Janis some help. Eliot can call in a doctor."

They swept through the massive gates that lay open to the homestead. There was fresh urgency in Cal's manner. "We need a nanny back for Marcus. You've been wonderful, but that's not your job. I have no option but to get back to the men. We're coming into our busiest time and I have outstations to check on yet. God, what a mess!" His tone was a mixture of grief and contempt.

CHAPTER TEN

As soon as Amber walked into the house she veered off to make her routine check on Marcus.

"He's outside, love," Dee told her. Dee was busy punching down dough to get a good even texture for her bread. In the time Amber had been on the station she had enjoyed all sorts of Dee's delicious, freshly baked breads and rolls. The woman never stopped but she obviously thrived on and took a great deal of pride and pleasure in running the household.

"Asleep?" Amber asked.

"Sleepin' his head off," Dee confirmed. "I guess he would after such a helluva night."

"And Janis?"

"Madam hasn't stirred as yet," Dee told her dryly. "I reckon she'd feel a whole lot better if she got some decent tucker into her."

"And Eliot?"

"He's with the baby." Dee had taken to whispering. "If this keeps up he could be a good candidate for a heart attack."

"Don't say that!" Amber shuddered. "I'll go out to them."

"I'll make coffee. I'll just shape this into loaves and set it aside for a while."

"Lovely!"

"You got on pretty good with Brooke?" Dee called.

Amber turned back. "I liked her, Dee. I think she took the message that she had no future with Cal on the chin."

"Seems like it." Dee shrugged. "Big surprise there or she had the sense to recognise she was outclassed. But what about Mrs MacFarlane?"

"Oh, Dee!" For a moment they just stared at each other.

"Okay, love." Dee relented. "Pity you got drawn into this. On the other hand…" She left the rest unsaid. Their whole relationship had taken a conspiratorial direction.

The long covered porch to the rear of the kitchen area had been turned, of late, into a day nursery for Marcus. It was beautifully cool and a great deal of care had gone into achieving an atmosphere of simplicity and balance. A seated stone Buddha sat high on a tall decorative stone plinth. Today Buddha was holding a basket of freshly picked bougainvillea flowers. Clumping bamboos provided foliage, mixed with golden canes and kentia palms. Little Marcus was benefiting from the peace and serenity.

Eliot stood up. "Brooke got safely away?"

Amber smiled. "I do so admire her ability to fly a plane."

"You could learn if you wanted to. To be honest, I've never met a young woman so capable."

"Well, thank you. But how much are we born with, Eliot?" she asked wryly. "It's the luck of the draw."

"So far as I'm concerned, you've been very lucky," he said. "Shall we sit down?" He pulled out a wicker chair for her.

"I'll just take a peep at Marcus. Dee is making coffee."

"I'm so sorry for last night," Eliot said when Amber returned. "I don't believe I've ever felt so terribly ineffective. I can't seem to say the right thing or offer the comfort my wife needs."

"Get the doctor back," Amber suggested gently. "Forgive me if I'm overstepping the mark.

"How could you be overstepping the mark?" Eliot's expression was bleak. "You've been an enormous help. Jan and I had no right to ask it of you. You're here as Cal's guest."

Amber thought she had rarely seen a more tormented face. "Today would be a good time, if it could be managed. The right medication will help Mrs MacFarlane. Get her through a bad patch."

"Doctors have been here before, Amber," Eliot reminded her. "My wife has drained an enormous well of sympathy with her behaviour."

"Make the call," Amber urged.

"I will, my dear," Eliot promised, his face eerily calm.

When Cal saw the Super King Air fly over he knew the RFDS was coming in to land. He threw himself into the Jeep, determined to be back at the house in case of any trouble. How had he never picked up on Jan's feelings? How *could* she have developed such feelings when he had never given her the remotest encouragement? For God's sake, she was his uncle's *wife*. The whole thing was sickening. He couldn't think about it and do his job. The only thing that seemed to hold him in place was returning to the homestead to find Amber there. She had touched his life in every possible way. He could feel her all around him, in the very air he breathed. He'd never imagined he *could* feel about a woman like he felt for her. He had thought himself in love with Brooke. He had come very close to marrying her. Outback born and bred, Brooke knew and understood exactly what their life would be. Amber was right. The whole torment of the breakdown of his parents' marriage had never left his mind.

It was crucial for his own happiness to find a woman with the strength to face life on the land squarely. A brave woman he could love and trust. His life's partner. Wasn't she right under his nose? Could he possibly be that lucky? He had been allowing himself to dream of winning Amber's heart. But was it unwinnable? Even if he *could* win it, would the marriage survive the early days of high romance that had made his parents commit to each other in the first place? Or would the full force of *remoteness*, the epic struggles with drought and flood, give rise to feelings of being trapped in a world that took more than it gave?

Amber was a city girl. A beautiful, accomplished woman. Wouldn't it be madness to expect a woman like that to settle for a life on the desert fringe? So she wanted to write? She'd have plenty of peace and quiet, he thought ironically. That was if Eliot and Jan could save their marriage and move away. In all probability Amber would soon be getting offers to return to television. Come back, all is forgiven. The very idea of her going away shook him to the bone.

Romantic love was an agony, so elemental one was powerless to fight it.

He knew in his heart that his uncle's hasty marriage wasn't going to last. Where then did that leave an innocent child? The greatest blessing of all to most women had turned out to be a real calamity for Janis. Not all women were born to be nurturers. He had learned that the hard way.

Cal made the home compound in record time, parking the Jeep in the shade. His stomach muscles were knotted with tension. He wanted to turn away from all this; he had no option but to go forward. He was master of Jingala.

Dee met him in the entrance hall. Not Amber. Only the sight of her could ease his tension.

"How's it going?" He fixed Dee with a questioning stare.

"Doc Trowbridge has persuaded Mrs MacFarlane she needs a while being looked after in a clinic." Dee spoke without expression.

"Okay. That's good, is it?"

"Better than any of us thought. We expected resistance."

"So she's agreed, then?" There was no reason to doubt what Dee was saying, yet he felt enormously on edge. "Where's Amber?"

"She's upstairs," Dee assured him with a backward jerk of the head. "Eliot wanted her along. Poor man is right out of his depth. He'll travel back with Mrs MacFarlane, of course. By the sound of it, they're coming now."

Both of them looked up as a small group of people moved into view at the top of the timber staircase. Dr Tim Trowbridge—well known to them—and a nurse brought up the rear. Amber was a little in front of Eliot, who was gently leading his wife by the arm, an expression of great unhappiness on his face. Janis, on the other hand, looked mute and sullen, eyes dark in their sockets. What shocked Cal most of all was the fact that Janis had cut her long dark hair. No, not cut, she'd *hacked* it so it fell in jagged layers.

Cal moved very fast to the bottom of the stairs, his senses finely honed to all sorts of dangers, on full alert.

At the sight of him Janis suddenly erupted, shaking off her husband's hand with a single violent motion. "*She* did this," she shouted. "We were all right until *she* came."

While the others stood transfixed by this unexpected burst of rage, Janis swooped on Amber. Though thin, Janis was now possessed of a manic strength.

"Bitch! You won't have him." She locked her arms around Amber, thrusting her forwards to the very top of the stairs.

"Janis!"

"Mrs. MacFarlane!" Behind them startled cries rang out in horror and protest.

Only Cal had read Janis's mind. Off balance with jealousy and her perception of Amber as the enemy, Janis had been driven to act. He tore up the stairs as Janis, with unnatural strength, was attempting to push her intended victim down them. It was all happening too fast...

Amber had begun to resist strongly but, in the shocked interim, Janis had gained the upper hand. Janis pushed out with all her might, her expression so triumphant she might have been disposing of the one person who stood between her and all future happiness.

"There!" she shouted in triumph.

With sick terror Amber could feel herself go. She was falling…toppling… Even as it was happening, her brain flashed a picture of her prone body at the foot of the stairs. A tragedy, with Janis MacFarlane to blame. What a blot that would be on the proud MacFarlane name.

Feeling utterly disconnected, beyond help, Amber braced herself for the worst. A broken hand, a broken shoulder, a broken wrist, a broken neck? Only, instead of her fall continuing, it was interrupted on the way by a hard male body thudding into hers.

Cal.

He crossed strong arms around her, knowing he couldn't stop the momentum but fully prepared to take the worst of the fall. He had taken plenty of falls before. There was a trick to the rolling and he had long since learned it. Even so, something could always go wrong. He wasn't just saving himself, he was endeavouring to save the woman he loved. It only made things that much harder.

"Go with me, Amber!" he muttered urgently, not even sure if she heard him.

She did, allowing her body to go pliant. She was putting all her trust in Cal's ability to cushion their inevitable stunning descent.

Even Janis was momentarily silenced, taken in hand now by both her husband and Trowbridge, who was appalled and not bothering to hide it.

Cal hit the floor first, deadening the impact for Amber, who came to rest half slumped over his back. Her breath was rattling through her body with shock, but she knew with enormous relief that she had come out of it unharmed. Both of them just lay there, Cal winded. Amber was frantic that he might have taken a hard knock to the head. She tried to sit up to make sure he was all right, with Janis all the while at the top of the stairs shouting down at her, "I wish I'd killed you! I wish you were dead."

Truthfully, Amber was so grateful to be unharmed she called with black humour, "I'm doing my best!" If it hadn't been for Cal, Janis might have got her wish. Surely Janis hadn't planned it? Amber had to reject that. It had been an unpremeditated act. Janis needed a scapegoat for her perceived failure in life. Amber had been elected.

Cal, however, saw no humour whatever in the situation. He brought himself into sitting position, getting his breath and ignoring the stabbing aches and pains through his upper body and a worse one at the back of his head.

"Are you okay?" Amber begged him, her heart in her eyes. Incredibly, Janis, at the top of the stairs, was demanding to be released, as if she had done nothing wrong.

"I wouldn't have had you within a thousand miles of harm," he told her bleakly. "Now this. That performance was enough to last me my lifetime."

He rose to his feet a shade gingerly, bringing Amber with him but keeping her within the shelter of his arm. "I hope you find health and peace, Janis," he said. "I truly do. But you'll never set foot in this house again."

A sombre pall fell over the household for the rest of the day. Even the two house girls went about their chores hushed. No merry giggles resounded around the big open rooms. All was quiet. Even little Marcus didn't break the silence with a single cry for attention. It seemed that in the absence of his mother Marcus was turning into a model child.

How sad was that?

Even though Janis had intended her real harm, Amber couldn't find it in her heart to condemn the woman. Some part of her would always pity Janis MacFarlane, who was later to abandon the child she had given birth to without a backward glance. It was as though it had never happened.

Cal returned to work, a sombreness on him like a dark veil. He was devastated that real harm could have been done to Amber, and in his own home. He had accepted that Janis needed help, but never until those very last minutes had he come to the realisation she was an actual *danger* to the one woman she saw as a threat. In a way, it was all *his* fault. There must have been clues along the way but, all unknowing, he had missed them like a fool. Why hadn't Eliot hinted at the bizarre situation—probably paralysed with embarrassment—or at least taken Janis away whether she wanted it or not? Why had Eliot allowed Janis to call the shots? Was he trying to save his marriage? Eliot was only staving off the inevitable. This was a marriage that should never have taken place.

It shocked and humiliated him that Tim Trowbridge and his nurse had witnessed what had happened. It could easily have been a tragedy. A police investigation. Cal knew not a word of the incident would go any further, but that didn't stop him from agonizing over the whole terrible business. After that, Amber would surely be determined on going back home.

And who could blame her? She had come as close to serious assault as she was ever likely to in her life. He could see how it had shaken her, even though she had gazed quietly at him with tears glistening in her beautiful golden eyes. "Thank you, Cal. You saved me."

She might have been part of the family already, prepared to close ranks. That she had come so close to real danger while under his roof and his protection he found shattering. For the first time he confronted head on what he had been trying to keep within manageable limits.

If he lost Amber, he lost *everything*.

Dee was busy, ladling three teaspoons of sugar into Amber's teacup, her preferred antidote to shock. "She coulda killed ya!"

"Well, she didn't." Amber took a sip, face screwed up at the excessive sweetness. "Let that be an end to it."

"Good thing you feel like that. You're so forgiving!" Dee shook her head in wonderment.

"Cal can't forgive himself," Amber lamented.

Dee nodded. "He's taken it to heart. You were brought here as his guest, yet Janis and her troubles wrecked all that."

"No, Dee, I've loved being here. I love this place. I love the wilderness, this extraordinary desert environment. I love the way I can go riding any time I please. A dozen scenarios for a book having been filling my head. *We* get along so well." She reached out to take Dee's hand. "I love little Marcus—I pray things will work out for him. Eliot loves him. There could be light at the end of the tunnel for Janis."

Dee clicked her tongue in dissent. "You mark my words. When a bit of therapy gets her back on her feet, she'll file for divorce. Eliot will have to part with a few million. That should keep her going. It's a no-brainer who gets Marcus. Janis won't want him. I have an idea that's what the beef was with her mother. Her mother probably didn't want Janis, either. What Janis convinced herself she felt for Cal wasn't love. It was a *sickness*."

Amber set down her cup so quickly it rattled in the saucer. "And you knew all about it, Dee?"

Dee looked ashamed. "I had a struggle with it at first. Couldn't believe it. But it was in everything she said, the look in her eyes. She fell for him, hook, line and sinker. I reckon it was the first real bond of her life. No one was attractive to her but Cal. Not even her own baby. That's how bad it was. Fatal attraction."

"Oh, dear me, yes." Sadly Amber shook her head. "Cal hates the very idea of it. I think he's blaming himself."

"Well, then, you'd better talk to him," Dee said. "You care about him, don't ya?" She fixed Amber with her shrewd black eyes.

"What does it look like, Dee?" Amber gave this knowing woman a wry smile.

"Ask me, ya perfect for each other," Dee grunted, to cover a little sob.

Amber got away for her ride late afternoon. She could feel the kinks and twinges in her body from the fall. She wondered how Cal, who had taken the brunt of it, was faring. In all likelihood he had experienced far worse. A good gallop might straighten her out. Her whole being was too restless to remain at the homestead.

She took Horatio in preference to the mare. Horatio would test her. She felt like being tested. Janis MacFarlane's lesson in loving—or lusting—had been a harsh one. It had crushed love for her husband and, even more sadly, love for her baby out of existence. Amber couldn't shake off a sense of pity, not knowing then what she would learn in the future. She had no need to spend any time pitying Janis MacFarlane. Janis was destined to fall on her feet.

In the afternoon light the landscape was glowing with colour, all the brilliant dry ochres—burnt umber, cinnabar, chrome-yellow, black, white and charcoal—to complement the intense opal-blue of the sky. The Hill Country was washed with colours from another spectrum—the mauves, the soft purples, the grape-blues. High above them an eagle coasted, sometimes appearing to hover motionless. She knew the great wedge-tailed eagles made their eyries in the far-off hills with their prehistoric rock galleries she had yet to see. Once she spotted, to her delight, a group of kangaroos in company with almost as many emus, the emus stalking around majestically, as befitting giants of the bird world. The grace and freedom of these animals. She thought she could watch them all day. The great plains that at first seemed so empty were actually swarming with life. The bird life alone was beyond belief.

This was the real Australia. The Outback. The home of the cattle kings. She was hoping to get to ride that exotic beast, the camel. Hundreds of them were roaming the station. A camel could go anywhere and everywhere in the desert, comfortably travelling twice the distance even a big thoroughbred horse like Horatio could travel. Jingala had drawn her in to the point she felt she would have difficulty in letting go. She had thought she would be visiting one of the world's harshest environments, an immensity of *brown*. What a surprise she'd been in for! She hadn't been privileged to see the miracle of the wild flowers, although swathes of paper daisies still lingered across certain sections of the station. Jingala wasn't the desert proper. It bordered the real desert, the Simpson, fifty-six thousand square miles of rolling red sand dunes. In her receptive frame of mind she felt a close affinity with this ancient land. She would have no difficulty in making it her home.

Returning to the homestead, the beauty of the sunset once more held her spellbound. No wonder the aborigines worshipped the land. It had such power—power to ease the mind. She felt immeasurably better after her ride. Jingala homestead was extraordinary, set down as it was in an oasis of green, with no sign of human habitation to all points of the compass. She could understand the desolation Cal's mother must have felt. Outback life had proved unliveable in the end to a woman who had been at war with her environment. She understood too how Cal, suffering the experience of his mother's abandonment, had settled, whether consciously or unconsciously, on Brooke Rowlands for a wife. His main priority would have been to choose a woman he could hold onto. A woman who had been reared to Outback life. Sexual desire would have been necessary, but Brooke was very attractive with a charming way to her. She had been very good with little Marcus, too. Holding him in a way he'd responded to and liked. She didn't think Brooke was actually promiscuous. She had probably been having fun, had too much to drink and fell into bed with a young man she knew well. Brooke would have realized her dreadful mistake the instant she'd woken up.

Alas, too late!

Cal demanded total emotional commitment. Asking another woman to marry him would involve considerable practical and emotional risks. Was he ready to take the chance? In the time she had been on Jingala they had discovered they had a lot in common. Not just the powerful sexual attraction that gathered strength with every passing day. The question of when they would come together was like a constant crackle in the atmosphere.

It had been Janis MacFarlane's unstable behaviour that had piled on the pressure. It hadn't been a normal holiday; or a normal getting to know one another. Far from it. She was happy with the way she had gained Cal's respect. Her fear now was that recent events would cause him to retreat, at least for a period of time before he took any final step. He had to see her not just as a desirable woman. He had to see her as the *right* woman. She had to live up to what he wanted in his life's partner.

Her own feelings had settled into absolute certainty. She loved him. Her search for her soulmate had come to an end. Cal MacFarlane was a man she was ready to love, honour and obey. She was comfortable with all three.

* * *

From habit, she entered the office to check whether she had any emails. She had received quite a few from Zara that made her smile. Zara was one of the few people who knew where she was. They'd had great times together. Only one message came up. She eased herself into the leather desk chair to read it.

Greetings, Amber!
Your friend Zara parted with your email address. The price—she wants a job—could find her a spot. As for you, I'm delighted to hear you're having such a great time. Might be an idea if you got an interview out of the MacFarlane Cattle King. I remember the shot of the two of you coming out of that restaurant. You looked like a couple of movie stars. You'll be heartened to hear scores of angry viewers have been inundating the station with emails demanding to know when we're going to put you back on air. You're loved, kiddo! Erskine is a decent enough guy after all. Word has come down from on high, you're free to come home. We've all missed you. Even Jack. He and Liv Sutton aren't making it as the dream team. He thinks she's a lightweight. She thinks he's a pain in the ass. So Jack is ready for your return. Please let me know when that great day will be. Make it real soon but give me time to arrange a welcome home party.
All my best,
Paddy

When she was done reading it, Amber printed it off, then read it once more, all the while quietly muttering to herself. Instead of being thrilled, as she would have been under normal circumstances, she felt hugely unsettled. She couldn't ignore

Paddy. She would have to answer him. What would she say? She'd take the next plane?

How unexpected was life! Today, of all days, yet another emergency had been forced on her. What was she supposed to do? Hand Cal the email? Let him read it, digest the contents, then make a telling comment?

What would she do if he handed back the email with the casual enquiry, *So when are you thinking of leaving?*

Depending on the way he said it and the accompanying look in those enigmatic green eyes, she might have to answer, *On the first flight available.*

She had no idea what she would do if he took her imminent departure in his stride. Probably tear her hair out. But surely tearing her hair out would come close to Janis's hacking off *her* locks? Was it a female thing? One of the ultimate expressions of grief?

For the first time Dee insisted Marcus spend the night with her. "The nanny will be flying in tomorra and you need a break," she told Amber in a no-argument voice.

"My TV station wants me back, Dee," Amber confessed.

"Wh-a-t?" Dee fell back as if she'd been shot.

"There was an email waiting for me. The viewers miss me."

"We'll be missin' you too." Dee started to pull frantically on an ear lobe. "What are you gonna do? Sorry, it's none of my business, love."

"I think it is." Amber moved to hug her. "I'll tell Cal over dinner, but I'm worried how he'll react. He mightn't care as much about me as I'd like to think." It came out *so* forlornly.

"Tell him all the same," Dee advised.

Towards the end of dinner Cal suddenly grasped Amber's narrow wrist. "What's on your mind?" His tone was sharp and alert.

"You think there's something on my mind?" Madness to deny it.

"Amber, don't let's get into that question for question stuff," he warned. "Are you sure you're feeling okay?" His eyes swept over her. She was wearing a short dress with little ruffles in a shade almost the colour of her hair. She looked beautiful, if sad.

"I told you, Cal, just a few twinges here and there. You're the one who took the brunt of it."

"It's my job to look after you." His mouth faintly twisted.

She had to glance away to cover her emotional agitation. Another beautiful desert night, a dazzling canopy of stars. All her nerves bunched. Unsure what to tell him. Terrified he would take her news calmly, thus crushing her hopes.

"*Tell* me," he said in that clipped tone he used to express displeasure. "You want to go home. You want to go back where you belong."

"And you're going to let me go?"

His light eyes darkened. "I know, apart from Janis and the whole situation, you've been enjoying yourself here. But you have the whole world at your feet. You're as much out of your element as a yellow rose springing from a desert rock."

She leapt to her own defence, temper flaring. "Aren't you the one who told me about all the exquisite little wild flowers that manage to survive growing out of rocks? I'm no hot-house flower."

"No, you're a species of your own."

"A hardy one, I'd like you to know. Does this mean I should start packing?" Without meaning to, she found herself standing, more overwrought than she knew. "That's enough to send me home."

He stood as well, his expression intense. "I thought you said you wanted to go?"

"I said no such thing. Here, read this." She turned about to snatch up the email she had left folded on the carved console.

"I don't need to read it." He took it all the same. "You've

told me all I need to know. They want you back. I knew they would. You're obviously very valuable to them."

"It was your wicked old grandfather who gave the okay," she said, conscious there was too much heat in her voice. "Does he know I'm here?"

"Who cares what he knows," Cal responded bluntly. "Seems like the trip is over and the crying begins."

"I don't see *you* crying," she accused, furious to feel the sting of tears at the back of her eyes.

"Not now, anyhow," he said with heavy humour. "Are you going to sit down again? We haven't finished dinner. Dee will be upset."

"You should have waited until *after* dinner," she said, lowering herself back into the rattan armchair.

"I wish I had," he said wryly, taking the chair opposite her. "What do you want from me, Amber?"

"What do you want from *me*? Let's get it on the table." She reached for her half empty wineglass, tossing the contents back. She must have learned that from Janis.

"Well, I'm mad to make love to you," he announced in a don't-push-me-too-far voice. "I'm not going to pretend about that. It's chronic by this stage. I don't think I can last another day without having you. Are you taking me seriously? You should."

"Okay, then. You've cited desire." She ticked off a finger. "Kindly explain what else, if anything, makes me attractive to you."

"Don't start this, Amber," he begged, like a man fast reaching his limits. "Don't, don't, *don't*."

"Annoying you, am I?" Her golden eyes flashed.

"Inciting me, more like it. As if you didn't know. Maybe we can sleep together tonight, then pretend it never happened?"

She tried to breathe steadily. Couldn't manage it. "Apologise for that."

"No." His answer was blunt. "You might like to calm down,

though. Dee's coming with the coffee. She told me she's taking care of Marcus tonight."

Sure enough she fired. "Does that mean we're free to give in to our desire?"

"Well, I've been considering it if you haven't," he returned sardonically. "In some ways I regret my inability to withstand you."

"Of course you do," she said. "You much prefer to maintain a distance."

"That's what's kept me from knocking your door down."

He looked as if he meant it. "Ah, so you're a caveman? You've been keeping that from me. Anyway, here's Dee," she warned as Dee wheeled the trolley into the room. "She's within earshot. I don't want her to see us fighting."

"Is that what we're doing?" he asked with a lift of the brow. "You know I pictured something quite different for tonight. But nothing is certain in life."

"You can say that again!"

They called it a night before the two of them worked up a *real* argument.

"I'd really appreciate it if you'd let me stay until Eliot comes home and Marcus is responding well to the new nanny" was Amber's parting shot. Extremely unfair because he hadn't said a thing about her leaving. Over-emotional with the events of the day, she was in a perverse mood, deliberately provoking him.

"*Former* nanny," he corrected shortly. He stood in the entrance hall, watching her flounce up the stairs with those long beautiful legs. "She was here when Jan was ringing the changes. She's a very nice woman—widow, early forties, ex-nursing sister, Martha Fenton. She was handling Marcus just fine only Janis swore an oath to get rid of her, just like her predecessor."

"And me!" Amber reminded him. "Never a kind word. Goodnight, Cal." She clipped the words off in a tone she had perfected from him.

"You're not going to your martyrdom, are you?" he called after her in a dark, sardonic voice.

"I'm trying not to charge down the stairs and hit you." Every electrical circuit in her blood was hot-wired.

Cal gave a short laugh. "And what do you think would happen if you did?" Desire was shooting through his body like a flaming arrow, but he tried to bank it down. She could flounce off tonight. It had been a terrible day for her. But he knew, beyond all denial, he would never let her go. Lock her up if he had to. The sun shone more brightly with Amber around.

She paused to look down at him. His green eyes glittered brilliantly, but his handsome features looked unusually drawn. Her breath caught. "I thought you were trying to put the brakes on, not play with fire?" She hesitated uncertainly.

"I've never stopped playing with fire with you around." He gave that twisted smile. "Go to bed, Amber. Try to get a good night's sleep. It's been one hell of a day. I'm sure you'll agree."

"Oh, I do!" To her absolute horror she found herself close to tears. Once more her life was running off the rails. And serve her right! There was always something to cause fresh pain. Sean had hurt her pride. This was the kind of pain that went on for ever.

"We'll talk again," he promised.

She spun in a passion, a single tear sliding her cheek. "Thanks a lot."

"Well, it's a good thing, isn't it, our talking?" he appealed to her.

"Oh, talk, talk, talk!" she burst out over the lump in her throat. "Why can't you embrace life, Cal? There are worse things than trusting a woman. Even one with red hair. The trouble with you is you're *frightened* to reach out."

"Am I?" he asked crisply.

She ignored the hard challenge. "Of course you are."

"We'll see about that."

To her shock, he started to come after her. There was only one thing to do. *Run!* Though exactly why she was running perplexed her. Maybe it was another weird insight into female behaviour. Her heart pounding, tremors running up and down her arms and legs, she reached her bedroom door. She had left it open when she had gone down to dinner, so she was able to fly through the door, slamming it after her.

The speed with which he arrived at her door was like a jolt to the heart. "Open the door, Amber," he commanded.

That got to her. No plea. An *order*. "I'm locking it," she cried. Even to her own ears her voice sounded wild. Lock the man out of his own house?

"Like who owns this house—*you*?"

"You seem to have forgotten I'm your guest."

"Guests don't usually start lecturing their hosts," he called back. "Open up, before I break it down."

"Suit yourself." He wouldn't break down his own beautiful timber door. That would be a crying shame.

Silence. Oh, Lord! He must have gone away. She had to be a basket case because she was terribly, terribly disappointed. Dispiritedly, she collapsed on the side of her bed, trying to calm down. Her heart had been racing in delicious terror; now she waited for it to slow. She could have handled this differently. Why hadn't she? Didn't he know how much she loved this life? He damned well *did*. She had no fears of the remoteness. What the heck was her job, anyway? Reading the news. What was the enormous satisfaction in that? She wanted a *life*. She wanted kids. She wanted to write. She wanted *him*. Surely he could see the sort of woman she was?

There were footsteps along the outside veranda. Heavy,

purposeful footsteps. How the heck had he got up there? She leapt up from the bed, ready for anything.

"So you want to play. Is that it?" He was framed by the open French windows. He looked extraordinarily masterful, all strength and dominant sexuality.

"How did you do that?" she asked with some wonder. He had a few green leaves caught in his thick crow-black hair.

"Good question."

"You climbed a tree?" Her voice was shaking with excitement.

"How else would I do it?" His brilliant eyes ranged over her. Her lovely face was surrounded by her bright cascading hair. It swirled over and around her shoulders. There was a high flush in her cheeks from excited blood. "I thought I was right," he said. "You're crying."

"So what?" She dashed the sparkle of tears away. "I'm good at it too when I get started. Sometimes tears are outside a woman's control, didn't you know?"

"And sometimes a man can hurt a woman when he doesn't intend to." Emotion deepened his voice. "Look at me, Amber."

Look at him! She was desperate to *run* to him but uncertainty continued to pin her in place.

"All right, if Mahomet won't come to the mountain, the mountain must come to Mahomet."

"Oh, Cal what are we doing?" Even as she said it, her body was up and swaying towards him. She was in a high state of arousal. Her sensitive nipples had already tightened into buds that desperately needed the touch of Cal's forefinger and callused thumb.

"Nothing as yet," he gritted, hauling her into his arms. "Just let yourself go. All you have to do is hold onto me."

His dark head blocked out the overhead light. She breathed in his warm breath. "But Cal, I need to know—"

He cut her off. "Ask me afterwards. I know what you want.

I know what *I* want. Let our bodies do the talking for us." He brought up his right hand, weaving his long fingers into the loose mass of her hair. "Open your mouth."

Her mind went clear of everything but *want*. She could feel her limbs dissolving. Her body was as alight as if a fire blazed inside. She could have wept from the conflagration. She did in fact make a little sound that could have been interpreted as dissent, only Cal was having none of it. He lowered his mouth over her cushiony lips, kissing her so deeply, so voluptuously that her arms came around him, tightening, pulling him in to her as if she would never let him go.

Surely that settled everything, he thought, moving into a high state of elation. She tasted wonderful. Like peaches and sunshine. Their tongues were meeting, mating, in a sinuous love dance. He could feel her supple fingers begin to knead his back. She seemed desperate to touch not fabric but *skin*. He understood perfectly. He had only to release a zipper to have her satiny dress slip from her body and pool at their feet. His hands moved compulsively to the undercurves of her beautiful breasts, taking their weight, his fingertips centring on the rose-coloured nipples. He could see the agitated flutter of her eyelids. He already knew she wasn't wearing a bra, so it would be naked flesh he would find beneath his hand.

Once he fell to kissing and caressing her he couldn't stop. But neither was she stopping him. She was giving him everything he so desperately desired. It was all out in the open. The passion they shared for one another couldn't be denied. Something this powerful demanded trust. He was ready to embrace it. There was wisdom in listening to her…

Gradually their lovemaking escalated to a pitch where it was hard to tell what was teasing and what torture. Still holding her, he stripped back the quilted silk coverlet of the bed, urged on by the soft little mewing sounds she was making.

"I love you," she cried frantically. She couldn't hold it in. Her whole body was vibrating with it.

He all but tossed her onto the bed in his urgency. "Yes, I know." He began to strip his splendid body naked, the lamplight gilding his skin.

"You *know*?" She half rose up from the bed, then fell back again, transfigured by his words.

"Of course I know," he said in a voice pent-up with emotion. "I think we've pretty well cleared that small point up."

"Then I'm waiting to hear you tell me you love me." Ecstatically she threw her arms back over her head, inviting the adoration that was emblazoned on his dynamic face.

"I plan to." He half loomed over her, all strength and sinew and rippling muscle. "But it's going to take hours—" long kisses "—and hours…"

Rapture shone from her face, resounded in her soul. "So you don't want me to go away?"

His green eyes were impossibly brilliant. "There's one thing I haven't told you yet, my beautiful Amber. You want me to say it, right?"

She pulled him down bedside her, spooning her body into his, welcoming his powerful arousal. "I'm listening."

"I want to tell you something I haven't told another soul." He gathered her even closer, binding her to him as if by invisible chains.

"Yes?" she whispered, shaking with excitement, her thighs already moving apart.

"I'm ready to reach out. It was you who worked that miracle. I see a woman so beautiful, so strong, so full of character, I worship at her feet. I see a woman I will love for as long as I live. I see a woman I can trust. I love you, Amber. I adore you. I'm not letting you get away. I'm going to keep you for ever and ever."

Saying it, he reached down to capture her yearning mouth.

* * *

And so it turned out. A lifetime of sharing, fiery little clashes, passionate making up, the maintaining of a dynasty. Three children in total. A boy and girl of their own. Steven first, then Stephanie named in honour of their grandmother, who often came to visit. Their cousin, Marcus, more a big brother than a cousin, was raised as part of this loving brood. Janis MacFarlane never remarried but she did reach dizzy heights in the world of finance. She became CEO of a merchant bank, which gave her absolute fulfilment. Eliot MacFarlane eventually found true love. He married his son's former nanny, Martha Fenton, a woman as gentle and loving as his first wife, Caro. Amber wrote her books to critical acclaim.

It was a great life. A total life. A life to shout about!

We'll be spotlighting a different series
every month throughout 2009
to celebrate our 60th anniversary.

**Look for Harlequin® Superromance®
in September!**

*Celebrate with
The Diamond Legacy
miniseries!*

Follow the stories of four cousins as they come to terms
with the complications of love and what it means to
be a family. Discover with them the sixty-year-old secret
that rocks not one but two families.

A DAUGHTER'S TRUST by *Tara Taylor Quinn*
September

FOR THE LOVE OF FAMILY by *Kathleen O'Brien*
October

LIKE FATHER, LIKE SON by *Karina Bliss*
November

A MOTHER'S SECRET by *Janice Kay Johnson*
December

Available wherever books are sold.

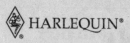

HARLEQUIN®

American ★ Romance®

The Ranger's Secret
REBECCA WINTERS

When Yosemite Park ranger Chase Jarvis rescues
an injured passenger from a downed helicopter,
he is stunned to discover it's the woman he
once loved. But Chase is no longer the man
Annie Bower knew. Will she forgive him for
the secret he's been keeping for ten long years?
And will he forgive Annie for her own secret—
the daughter Chase didn't know he had…?

*Available September
wherever books are sold.*

"LOVE, HOME & HAPPINESS"

www.eHarlequin.com

You're invited to join our Tell Harlequin Reader Panel!

By joining our new reader panel you will:

- Receive Harlequin® books—they are FREE and yours to keep with no obligation to purchase anything!
- Participate in fun online surveys
- Exchange opinions and ideas with women just like you
- Have a say in our new book ideas and help us publish the best in women's fiction

*In addition, you will have a chance to win great prizes and receive special gifts!
See Web site for details. Some conditions apply.
Space is limited.*

To join, visit us at
www.TellHarlequin.com.

REQUEST YOUR FREE BOOKS!
2 FREE NOVELS PLUS 2
FREE GIFTS!

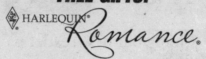

HARLEQUIN *Romance*

From the Heart, For the Heart

YES! Please send me 2 FREE Harlequin® Romance novels and my 2 FREE gifts (gifts are worth about $10). After receiving them, if I don't wish to receive any more books, I can return the shipping statement marked "cancel." If I don't cancel, I will receive 4 brand-new novels every month and be billed just $3.84 per book in the U.S. or $4.24 per book in Canada. That's a savings of at least 15% off the cover price! It's quite a bargain! Shipping and handling is just 50¢ per book.* I understand that accepting the 2 free books and gifts places me under no obligation to buy anything. I can always return a shipment and cancel at any time. Even if I never buy another book, the two free books and gifts are mine to keep forever.

114 HDN EYU3 314 HDN EYKG

Name	(PLEASE PRINT)	
Address		Apt. #
City	State/Prov.	Zip/Postal Code

Signature (if under 18, a parent or guardian must sign)

Mail to the Harlequin Reader Service:
IN U.S.A.: P.O. Box 1867, Buffalo, NY 14240-1867
IN CANADA: P.O. Box 609, Fort Erie, Ontario L2A 5X3

Not valid to current subscribers of Harlequin Romance books.

**Are you a subscriber of Harlequin Romance books
and want to receive the larger-print edition?
Call 1-800-873-8635 today!**

* Terms and prices subject to change without notice. Prices do not include applicable taxes. Sales tax applicable in N.Y. Canadian residents will be charged applicable provincial taxes and GST. Offer not valid in Quebec. This offer is limited to one order per household. All orders subject to approval. Credit or debit balances in a customer's account(s) may be offset by any other outstanding balance owed by or to the customer. Please allow 4 to 6 weeks for delivery. Offer available while quantities last.

Your Privacy: Harlequin Books is committed to protecting your privacy. Our Privacy Policy is available online at www.eHarlequin.com or upon request from the Reader Service. From time to time we make our lists of customers available to reputable third parties who may have a product or service of interest to you. If you would prefer we not share your name and address, please check here. ☐

HR09R

**Stay up-to-date
on all your romance
reading news!**

The Harlequin
Inside Romance
newsletter is a **FREE**
quarterly newsletter
highlighting
our upcoming
series releases
and promotions!

Go to
eHarlequin.com/InsideRomance
or e-mail us at
InsideRomance@Harlequin.com
to sign up to receive
your **FREE** newsletter today!

Coming Next Month

Available September 8, 2009

This fall, curl up and relax with a Harlequin Romance® novel!

#4117 KEEPING HER BABY'S SECRET Raye Morgan
Baby on Board
Cameron's from the richest family in town. Diana's pregnant, unwed and
definitely unsuitable. But will it stop these old friends from falling in love?

#4118 CLAIMED: SECRET ROYAL SON Marion Lennox
Marrying His Majesty
A year ago, Lily accidentally became pregnant with Prince Alexandros's
baby. Now Alex wants to claim his son. Will Lily agree to *Marrying His
Majesty?* Find out in the first book of this new trilogy!

#4119 EXPECTING MIRACLE TWINS Barbara Hannay
Follow surrogate mom Mattie's *Baby Steps to Marriage...*in the first of
a new duet by Barbara Hannay. How can Mattie begin a relationship with
gorgeous Jake when she's expecting twin trouble?

#4120 MEMO: THE BILLIONAIRE'S PROPOSAL Melissa McClone
9 to 5
When Chaney finds herself back working with billionaire playboy
Drake, she must remember how he broke her heart, *not* his devastating
charm... Oops!

#4121 A TRIP WITH THE TYCOON Nicola Marsh
Escape Around the World
Join Tamara as she travels through India on a trip of a lifetime, and
catch the fireworks when she bumps into a blast from her past, maverick
entrepreneur Ethan.

#4122 INVITATION TO THE BOSS'S BALL Fiona Harper
In Her Shoes...
Watch in wonder as this plain Jane is transformed from pumpkin to
princess when she's hired to organize her boss's company ball...and
dance in his oh-so-delicious arms!